IN THE CLOUD

A CLARKE LANTHAM MYSTERY

In The Cloud
A Clarke Lantham Mystery
by J. Daniel Sawyer

AWP Mystery
A division of ArtisticWhispers Productions

Book Design by ArtisticWhispers
Digital painting "Blood in the Creek" © 2015 J. Daniel Sawyer

Dedication

For Merlin
Who does with code what Lantham does with cars and guns

11:40 AM, THURSDAY

DAYS LIKE THIS, I'D KILL for a phone. Or a good clean piece of gauze. I've already killed someone for less today, and if I'm serious about seeing sunset, I'm going to have to kill again, maybe more than once, whether I want to or not.

I don't like killing people. But this...

These I want. Bad enough to taste it.

And I've got about three minutes before I get my shot.

It's not my fault. If Rachael hadn't run out on me six months ago, I wouldn't even be here. Sure as hell wouldn't be here alone. Don't know why she did it. She was the best assistant I've ever seen, and we were just getting the bugs worked out.

But one day she's saving my life and helping me nail the bad guys, the next day I've got Nya—she's my other assistant, the one that *doesn't* quit on her friends in a snit—waking me up, telling me she's dropped off the map.

We looked for her for weeks, too. Every damn place. Nya watched the police reports from the whole country. I called other PIs. We tracked her cell. Her bank account. I questioned her family. If there was a trick in my bag, I pulled it out and used it to find her.

The kid was just too good. I knew that one day she'd learn all I had to teach her and strike out on her own, and I knew when she did that I'd be in trouble—but I thought the trouble was going to come from competition when she set up an office across the street, not this kind of trouble.

This kind of trouble I can do without. If I never spend another morning trying to stop myself from bleeding out from a gunshot wound, it'll be too soon. And if Rachael hadn't done her little disappearing act, and felt guilty about it, I wouldn't be sitting on the floor of this abandoned stable hoping to hell I'd played my cards right so these two candidates for mercenary-of-the-year would walk in from the right direction.

"Lantham. Lantham!" The guy hissing in my ear calls himself Jerry, for reasons I'd rather not find out about. If I'd been given a name like that at birth, I'd have given it back and asked for a refund.

Maybe that's not fair. Maybe I'm bitter. Hot lead injections tend to make me edgy when they don't make me dead first.

"Shut up," I hissed at him.

"But..."

I shot him a look that made him turn shock white, which is a hell of a trick when the ambient skin tone is just half a shade away from coal-black.

Then I heard it too. A crunch from the path. Could be a deer. Could be a man. Could be a pair of men with big guns.

I needed to get back to the cars. There were cops back

there. Answers too, I hoped. I'd stashed a bagful of evidence near where Francine—that's what Rachael called my Subaru, for reasons I'd prefer to forget—near where Francine got run off the road. If I could make it back there, I might figure out what the hell this morning's madness is all about. Might even get some backup. But before I could do that, I had to do an end-run around the guys hunting us.

And keep the bloody civilians quiet.

This guy? One of my tag-alongs. I stashed the other one a ways down the hill inside a burned-out redwood. The two of them ran me off the road, though they swear it wasn't their fault, and I'm inclined to believe them. They're not smart enough to stage an accident like that. Or, not smart enough in the right way.

And they are *not* the kind of people you leave to fend for themselves when there are other people running around who are good at what they do. People who kill other people, on a professional basis.

People like those two out there in what was left of the fog.

People like me.

But this isn't my fault. This one is all on Rachael. And if I ever get my mitts on her again, I'm going to strangle her till her goddamn eyes pop out, and not even Nya's going to be able to stop me. Cause I've had it with her shit, and I'm gonna make damn sure she finds out if it's the last thing I do.

First, though, I gotta get out of here alive.

5:00 AM, THURSDAY

FIRST THING'S FIRST, THOUGH. The car crash didn't hurt me much. Wish I could say the same for Francine. She isn't making it out of the insurance adjuster's office alive.

I pulled two people out of the Jeep before I took a look underneath and got an idea of exactly how screwed I was.

Another car crash, Lantham? Really? I hear you ask. *You know you're a detective, not a stunt driver, right?*

Yeah, I know. If Rachael was here, she'd say it so you don't have to: I need another job. I really really *really* need a job that doesn't eat cars. This is the third time in the last couple years that my ride wound up on the wrong end of a physics equation.

Okay, yes, technically, the last one was my fault, because I was busy cracking a case when I should have been worried about why the road was serving venison sashimi on the hoof, but that's the only one. The other one, the one in Seattle? That wasn't my fault. Getting broadsided at a stoplight is pretty much the definition of "not my fault."

And this one? This is all Rachael's fault. If it wasn't for her, I wouldn't have had to run Highway 84 on an emergency call from her father, and I wouldn't have wound up stuck underneath a 1985 Jeep Cherokee with the front wheel poking through my windshield.

My insurance broker is going to kill me.

Maybe I oughta back up.

Three hours before, I got a call. The kind of call that rips you out of the warm arms of your bed and the gorgeous woman beside you. Well, in my case, it was a puppy with gigantism named Klepto. He was occupying Erica's normal spot, since she's off on assignment with her FBI unit somewhere in the wilds of Need-to-Know, And-You-Don't, USA.

Which is probably just as well. As much as I hate it when her boss calls her in the middle of the night, she hates it ten times as much when mine calls me—especially since my "boss" the last few months is Rachael's father, who's suddenly decided to adopt me as his personal pet project. He won't say why, but it doesn't take a genius to figure it out. When my absconded acerbic assistant left in a lather over she-wouldn't-say-what for god-knows-where just after fixing the business part of my business, she felt guilty.

You underestimate that woman's guilt-fetish at your peril. I learned that one the hard way before she left.

Thing is, Rachael's got a finely developed sense of justice. If she's going to screw you over, she does something to make up for it, unless she figures you had it coming. Not long after she disappeared, her dad started hiring me to do mop-up work for the Santa Clara County Sheriff Department. She put him up to it, I'd bet my boots, which is why this is her fault.

That was him on the phone. Not the kind of voice I want to wake up to.

"Lantham," he gravels, "I've got a discreet transport job for you. Meet me in the Starbucks parking Lot in Monta Loma Plaza in eighty minutes."

"Mountain View? That's a little out of your sandbox, isn't it?"

Well, it was. He gruffed that he wasn't gonna be arresting anyone, and went on about how I ought to be glad he was meeting me half way—then got all cryptic about it when I pointed out I was in Castro Valley and halfway would be at McCarthy Ranch.

Well, the job paid five hundred bucks, and if you can say no to five hundred bucks for two hours work, you're a hell of a lot richer than I am.

That time of morning, you can do Castro Valley to Mountain View in under an hour, so I rolled my sorry ass out of bed, gave it a quick scrub-n-rinse.

I hopped in Francine and chucked her shifter into reverse, backed out. Out in the middle of that empty street, with my ride pointed toward the freeway, I was looking right at Rachael's place. Nya was staying there almost full time now, just to keep it alive. Ostensibly she lives here, since she's more-or-less my adopted niece, but she and Rachael had a thing, and she's took the separation even harder than I have. She only comes home during the day, to work, anymore. Makes the house kinda lonely when Erica isn't around, what with just me and the mutt to fill up that big place.

This is the kinda job I'd have taken Rachael along on. Good long drive, lots of time to talk shop. The fact that she wasn't here pissed me off so much I couldn't see straight.

"Goddammit, Rache, where the fuck have you gone?" I punched the accelerator and left four-wheels of rubber on the tarmac.

At least the engine upgrades still worked.

"HERE." CAL DIDN'T BOTHER to order coffee, he just walked in and flopped a sealed envelope about three feet thick down on the table in front of me.

"Not gonna get coffee?"

"Nobody buys coffee. You can only rent it." Cal Oldman's not what you would call a personable guy. He's friendly enough, and he knows how to talk to people, but the right word for him is "decent." He's decent in the way that old veterans and some old cops are decent—they might kill you, or beat you into a coma, or buy you dinner, but they'll do it honestly, and they won't bullshit you in the pinch. Just don't expect them to be all shiny and smiley, even when you think they ought to be. You wind up on the wrong end of enough guns—or bureaucracies—and you figure out that not everyone is worth the effort. You've got a job to do, and people that get in the way can go play craps with Satan.

"What's this? Lost Michner epic?"

"If you were supposed to know that, it wouldn't be

sealed." Yeah, Cal wasn't having a good day either.

"This is a new side to your personality."

"Eh. Give me a minute." He got some coffee, came back. Guess he was thirsty after all.

"So what's the deal?"

"I need you to get this into the hands of a guy name Gus Ferris, out at Camp Loma Mar on Pescadero Creek Road a few miles off Highway 84."

"There's this amazing thing they got around here—can't say I've ever used it myself—but I think they call it 'the mail.' They charge a hell of a lot less than five hundred bucks."

"Hmph." Cal snorted into his coffee. "Amazing nobody's shot you with a wit like that."

"Oh, they have, I'm just too mean to die. I'd show you my scars, but Erica'd get kinda jealous."

"You know, I'm finally starting to get an idea."

"Of what?"

"Skip it, not important. Look, you need to get going. This has gotta be in Ferris's hands in two hours."

"Which means you've got thirty minutes to get me up to speed."

"What part of 'confidential' don't you understand, Lantham?"

"Confidential investigator means I don't talk to anyone about your stuff without a court order. It doesn't mean you don't tell me what I'm up to."

Cal took a long sip of his coffee. "My word as a cop isn't good enough for you?"

"Don't take this the wrong way, Cal, cause you know

it's just professional. But you and I have both known a lot of cops, and we know what the word of a cop means—or doesn't. And you're a client, too, and if there's one thing I've learned, it's that you can't trust clients."

"What a wonderful world you live in."

"Yeah, well, the rent's cheap and I get to have a dog, so it ain't all bad." The coffee wasn't bad—not worth the five bucks I paid for it, but when you're in a hurry and getting a couple hundred bucks an hour... "It's been five months of these little black bag jobs. I think that's long enough, don't you?"

"It's an IA thing."

"How big?"

"Let's just say you're the only party I can be sure won't do an end run around me."

"And just leave it at that?"

"For now. I might have more for you later."

I picked up the envelope. "Anything else I might want to know about this?"

"Yeah."

"What?"

"Don't get pulled over with it."

"That bad, huh?"

"Depends on how well you like Tasers."

"Rachael tell you my favorite little club in the City?"

He arched an eyebrow, took another drink.

"Well, I guess I'd better get on the road." I took my coffee, and the envelope. Stood up. "You haven't heard from Rachael by any chance..."

He shook his head.

"Didn't think so."

TRAFFIC IN MOUNTAIN VIEW at six in the morning is like a diesel engine from the sixties: loud, slow, useless, and getting stuck behind it kind of makes you want to slit your own throat. I didn't have to wade through too much of it, only a few eons worth.

Okay, miles.

I tried listening to the news to pass the time, but if you've ever tried listening to the news, you know what kind of a mistake that is. Good news doesn't sell, so this morning all the local news and talk stations were wall-to-wall with police shooting this, dead civilian that, and—the two that really pissed me off—stories about kids whose dogs got shot by cops who were trying to prove they were hot shit. Because everybody knows that you're a big man when you pump Fluffy full of lead.

I saw way too much of this kind of shit when I was on the Oakland PD, but at least I never heard about it on the radio. Last year or so, this kinda thing's gotten way out of hand—or maybe the news was finally paying attention to it. Kinda hard to be happy or pissed when stories like that actually make it to air, you know?

Music stations didn't do any better—they were wall-to-wall ads and Morning Zoos, and guess what the Morning Zoos were talking about?

Yeah.

And traffic was too nasty for me to pair my phone while trying to shift and not get steamrolled, because I'd forgotten to turn on the bluetooth before I left the parking lot.

But what the road taketh away, the road giveth back. Once you get on 84 headed up into the mountains, our little tale turns from a tragedy of traffic-boredom into a beautiful symphony filled with light violins and electric guitars, and my little Francine was after-marketed to take those curves and sweet-talk 'em like they were made of candy.

As a way to finish up a beautiful relationship, it wasn't all that bad.

And I was getting paid well enough for the trip that I figured it was basically free money.

Turns out it was more of a free insurance deductible.

Coming around a particularly gnarly turn on Pescadero road a few miles off 84, I ran face-first into the thickest fog I've seen socking in the Peninsula in at least a year and a half. In the space of fifty yards, my visibility shrank from "longer than the road" to "just barely longer than my hood," which in a 2004 Subaru Outback is *not* all that long. The occasional vehicle coming the other direction didn't look so much like a car as like a set of soft, glowing snowballs of death.

Not that I've got any reason to be paranoid or anything.

Well, a little pastthe big hairpin on the far side of the San Macdonald, they did get too close. Those lights came around a corner, maybe twenty yards ahead, at the kind of speed that would make a cheetah wet his pants, and swerving all over the place like someone put axle grease on their tires. That's not a good way for a vehicle to look at the best of times. It's a worse way for it to look when it's something with a high center of gravity, like an '85 Jeep. It's even worse when it's on the same road you're on, and headed in your direction, and you're hemmed in by cliffs on either side.

At that point, your choices pretty much depend on how you answer the question "Hey, met any good religions lately?"

That Jeep wiggled and weaved like the guy behind the wheel was a gold medalist in last night's beer-chugging competition, then it gave up, crossed the line, and headed straight for my front bumper.

I did what you do when some lame-brain decides that your lane looks like a parking space: I tried to get out of the way. I cranked hard left. He took a hard right, to dodge me, but he didn't have as much grip as I did. On a slick road, in pea-soup fog, with no reaction time, that put me right at the edge on his side of the road, where gravity was most inconvenient, just before he got there. If I'd had another half-second, maybe three quarters, I'd have cleared the edge before he lumbered on top of me, and I'd just have had to worry about surviving a thirty-vertical-foot roll down into a creek bed down a pretty-steep hill.

No sweat, right? I mean, that's why I installed the roll cage.

But me and poor Francine didn't get half so lucky. We went over the lip, and the Jeep smashed down right on the hood, and the whole assembly just sort of skated away down the hill. Locked together with that thing's front wheel trapped on my dashboard about three inches from my face, we were the wrong shape to roll and our momentum was too screwy to point us in any particular direction anymore. So we slid.

And slid.

And slid.

And then I had to climb out into a creek with freezing water up to my ankles. Joy.

No injuries. Okay, okay, a little scrape on my right ring finger from where the Jeep's wheels came through the glass, but not much else. My health insurance company would be happy with me, at least. Not enough to make up for how pissed my auto insurance agent was gonna be, but you take what you can get in this line of work.

Rattled, though? You bet. You try going nose-to-nose with a set of Jeep tires and see how long it takes you to come all over with the shakes.

That's okay. The assholes who ran me off the road were in worse shape. One of them, the guy who was driving, had cracked his skull. He was about forty, maybe, kind of soft everywhere. Round face as severe as any boxer's. Said his name was Jerry. The other, a woman about the same age, name of Lynn, built like a runner. She'd Charlie-horsed her arm when she slammed against the side of the car, which she didn't want to believe, so she kept trying to move it and saying "ouch" a lot. Neither of them were walking completely straight, but they could walk. With any luck, neither of them would drop dead from a cerebral hemorrhage. Still, I figured it was probably better to get the paramedics out here, just to be on the safe side.

Jerry started going on and on about how sorry he was, and I tried to be polite, but he *had* just killed Francine, and I was a little upset about that.

"Look," I said, "I get it, okay? Just get your insurance card out and I'll call AAA to get us pulled out of here."

"Right, right, yes, sorry." He dug in his pocket for his wallet and phone, both of which seemed to be alive and well despite the slings and arrows of outrageously idiotic driving.

Who, exactly, thinks it's a good idea to play Formula One in a Jeep Cherokee, anyway? I'd expect that kind of crap from my nephew, or at least I would have when he was sixteen, but by the time you get to forty years old you're supposed to know better. If you didn't, and you spend any time in a car, you don't make it to forty. At least, not unless you're really, really lucky.

Jerry handed me his insurance card, then started trying to dial his phone. Not easy to do when your fingers are shaking like that.

I pulled my phone out. Jerry kept talking in a loop, saying "It wasn't my fault, it wasn't my fault, it wasn't my fault." Well, I didn't much care about that. He crossed into my lane, and anyone looking at the way the wreck wound up settling could see that in a heartbeat. As far as the law and the insurance was concerned, it was his fault and he'd have to pay up.

My phone wasn't bashed. It was happy to see me—or, at least, the picture of Sir Klepto the Maniac (my too-huge-to-be-realistic mutt) wrestling with Special Agent

Erica Ellis made me happy to see it—and after a couple polite fondlings it presented me with the dial pad. I dialed the trusty old roadside assistance number, stuck the handset to my ear.

The phone beeped at me, like it was annoyed.

I gave it a good hard dirty look. It claimed it didn't have any signal. I guessed it kinda figured, what with being that far down a ravine in the ass end of San Mateo county. No one at the phone company ever promised me they'd put up cell towers in places where people like me were dumb enough to go adventuring.

Jerry was having the same problem.

Well, Lantham, I hope you're ready for a good hike to find some signal.

"It wasn't my fault, dammit, it wasn't my fault..." Jerry was still in a loop. I was starting to get a little annoyed with him, but nothing about him indicated that he had any practice dealing with this kind of adrenaline poisoning.

"Jerry, relax." I risked patting him on the back. Lynn watched me, gratitude in her eyes, as if she'd been afraid he'd just keep winding himself up until he had a heart attack.

"You don't get it, you don't get it..."

"Okay, explain it to me." I kept my voice low, even. Reassuring. You have to, to keep the panic from spinning up. People in that kind of loop feed off tension, and until you've seen that particular someone under that kind of pressure, you don't know which way they'll jump when they go off the deep end.

"The brakes wouldn't work. I...they just g...g...gave out."

That got me. Like an ice grip on my testicles. After what happened to my brother, any time I get in a car with spongy brakes I wonder if someone's cut the brake line. It happened to my kid brother Sam, and it's one of those great ways to get away with killing someone, if you're careful.

"Mind if I take a look?"

"No, no, that's fine. Yeah, go ahead." He was sweating now. Beads of bubblewrap on his shiny brown crown.

"Do me a favor in the meantime?"

"What's that?"

"Sit down. Breathe. Relax a little bit. We're all okay."

He nodded. "Sure. Yeah."

Not much of a conversationalist. It had to be the panic. Judging by the way he was dressed, he had to be in either IT or finance—you get a few dim-bulbs in those professions, but not many. Assholes, sure, but you find assholes everywhere. Stupid people, not so much. Not like you find in my first chosen profession, anyway.

Not that I'm bitter.

I crawled under the Jeep and checked the brake lines. What I saw there told me everything I needed to know about what kind of day this was going to be.

"Uh, Lynn?" I figured it wasn't any use talking to Jerry till he'd worked through his adrenaline poisoning and had access to his brain again.

"What?"

"Have either of you pissed anyone off lately?" It

occurred to me after I asked that she might not know. She hadn't been driving, and they hadn't told me they were married or involved. They didn't have the kind of body language you'd expect from a couple, which I'd have noticed sooner if I hadn't been fighting a pretty powerful case of the shake s myself.

She answered with what as probably the worst possible thing to say at that particular moment. "Not yet."

I didn't want to know. I mean, I *really* didn't want to know. Not unless they were willing to pony up a nice chunk of change to retain my professional services in a hurry, and even then I wasn't sure I'd take the job. Clarke Lantham Investigations isn't exactly in the bodyguard business. Oh, I've done that kind of work from time to time, when it pays well, but there's always the none-too-flimsy chance that you'll wind up in the hospital. Doesn't happen all the time, not even most of the time, but it does often enough that I tend to charge a lot for the very, very few gigs I take in that line.

"What do you mean, 'not yet'?"

She didn't say anything. If I was her, I wasn't sure I would have in her place. I was looking up at a shredded tire, shredded by a blowout on the interior side wall, which itself looked like it had blown out when the whole brake cylinder assembly blew apart.

Blew apart? Yeah. Like exploded. Which is something brake cylinders can't normally do unless they're deliberately weakened. Rust, maybe. That happens sometimes. When that happens, they usually don't burst with enough strength to shred a tire.

Sometimes, though, they get weakened because some dingleberry straps a little shaped charge of C4 or Semtex or something else plastic and pliable, and then triggers it remotely by calling up a little wearable wristwatch computer he's wired in.

A few pieces of it had survived, dangling from the strap which was still duct-taped to the axle, proving once again that duct tape binds the universe together.

Days like this, I'd give a lot of money for a time machine that would let me turn back the clock to the moment before I said "Yes, I'd be happy to take the job."

I slid out from under the Jeep. I resisted the temptation to pull my guns out and check the load. I'd done that before I slid into the car this morning, didn't need the distraction. Someone who cared enough to do a professional job like that might care enough to send out a quality control team, to make sure the job got finished up all pretty.

"Jerry," I said, "Lynn. Can you guys run?"

Jerry said "Huh?"

"You're right. It wasn't your fault. The brakes failed, and you lost the front driver's tire." Pro-tip: never mention bombs to a civilian who's already shaken up. They tend to get twitchy. Always lead into it as gently as you have time for. "I'm betting it happened right after you hit a pot hole—and I'll bet you never saw the pothole."

"How did you know that?"

"Because it wasn't a pothole. Someone tried to kill you by blowing out your brakes."

They both stared at me like I'd just beamed down

from the Starship Enterprise.

Then, slowly, Lynn started to nod. "Palmer."

Jerry got a grim look on his face.

"What?"

"Dido Palmer. Our other partner. Why do you care?"

Well, here goes nothing. "Because I used to be a cop."
I produced my wallet, pulled out a card, handed it over.
"Clarke Lantham Investigations, now. I'm a PI. And I..."

I didn't get to finish that sentence. An engine rumbled
to a stop at the top of the hill, and two doors shut.

"Oh, thank God," Lynn said.

"Shut up." I drew my .45 and thumbed off the safety.

"Oh my god!" Jerry scrambled to get away. He,
naturally, headed up the hill, because that's the way
normal people think. Run from the gun. It's not logical,
it's instinct. You see something dangerous, you run away.
And since I was standing downslope from him, "away"
meant "up the hill."

"Lynn, grab him!" I tried to keep my voice low. In the
fog and the still air everything we said would roll right up
to whoever-it-was anyway.

"What?"

"Ah, fuck." I started after him myself, keeping my gun
at low ready. I grumbled as I passed, loud enough for her
to hear, "There's nothing up on the road to tell them
there was an accident."

Pop pop pop pop

A volley of 9mm shorts zipped past me. I know that
sound anywhere. You wind up on the pointy end of
enough firefights, you get to be able to tell what's

shooting at you by how the load sounds when it pops off.

They were shooting blind, so I didn't get any extra ventilation, lucky me. I caught up to Jerry and got my hand on his belt just when I heard the unmistakable rack of a Mossberg pump-action 12-gauge.

I yanked Jerry to the side and dragged him down the hill, staying as low as I could. He wasn't quiet about it.

The Mossberg boomed, and my left arm went all hot and numb where the buckshot winged me. Which is about how my luck normally runs.

AT THAT POINT, I WAS NOT interested in explaining myself. I also didn't see much point in being quiet. I pitched Jerry forward, down the hill, and hoped to hell he didn't crack his melon at the bottom.

Without him weighing down my bloody left arm, I could pivot, raise my right, and fire back. There was no way I'd hit anything—I couldn't even see shadows up at the road level—but I'd sure as hell make 'em duck.

I threw seven of my eight shots their way, then dropped the magazine and switched it, which turns out to be harder than it looks when your support arm is trying like hell to convince you it's had a buckshot overdose.

By the time I'd gotten the reload done, I was down at the creek and behind the cars.

I found Jerry and Lynn there, too. Good thing they had some sense to do that before I told them. Sometimes, you take a gamble on people wanting to stay alive and it pays off. Small favors and all that, right?

Their good sense only went so far. They'd hidden behind the body, which might block the shotgun, at least from range, but it won't do anything to stop a nine mil. I had to yank them up behind the front wheels. I wasn't gentle, but sometimes delicacy will get you killed.

Engine blocks, on the other hand, will stop damn near anything.

"Okay, boys and girls, keep your hands and arms and heads below the vehicles," I swatted at Lynn's legs, which were dangling out into the open, "Legs too, as the management can't be responsible for anything you might lose by dangling it out into the line of fire. We've got maybe a minute before they start shooting again, so listen up. I've got to get something out of the car, and then we're going to run."

"Run? Where?" Lynn hissed.

"Downstream."

"Why?" She did not sound happy about the idea.

Christ, I don't have time for this. "Because I have the only gun that's keeping you alive," I held it up right in front of her face so she wouldn't get confused about anything. I also didn't mention that I had the .357 snubbie around my ankle, mostly on principle: You never know when your backup'll come in handy. "Now get ready."

I was squatting so I had a prayer of staying low enough not to get my head shot off, not an easy thing easy when you're tall enough to loom over people recreationally. I crab-pivoted around them both, which is both less dignified and more painful than it looks. Quiet as I could, I opened the passenger door. The Jeep hadn't crawled up on Francine's roof, and it hadn't smashed her front pillars, so the door frames weren't buckled or bent. Right now, I was loving that roll cage and structural work

I had put in when I bought her.

I reached in, under the glove box, and keyed one of the stash doors open. I reached in and got my fingers around a rough-weave nylon belt. Reserve firepower. Two extra mags for the 1911 and two extra speedloaders for the .357, strung on a black nylon adjustable buckle-strap that I'd picked up at Big 5. Not exactly black tie, but hey, I was covered in mud and blood, so it'd add a touch of class and maybe keep me alive.

Adding that to what I was carrying on my body, that gave me a grand total of twenty-two rounds left for the .45 and eighteen for the revolver.

Forty shots is not a lot for a guerrilla fight, and this could go that way really damn fast. The thing about gunfights, the reason they eat through so many rounds, is that if you're not careful, you spend most of your lead trying to scare the other guy into keeping his head down, kind of like I'd just done with my first mag. Burns through ammo awful damn fast.

Pop pop pop.

The window above me shattered. *Time to get under cover, Lantham.* I took a guess at the angle and squeezed off a couple cannon blasts into the fog, then rolled back to behind the engine.

My ears were ringing like hell. I turned my back to the two civilians and dug into my ankle holster for the little canister that Nya insisted I start carrying, after she heard about what the audiologist said about my gunfire-heavy lifestyle.

Sixty-five db foam earplugs. They don't keep me from

hearing people, but they do cut down on the gunfire. I twirled 'em up and twisted 'em in, then I leaned back to the civilians. "On the count of three, run. Stay ahead of me. I'll keep them off your ass."

"Why are you doing this?" Jerry's voice came through the foam like a whisper in a tornado, but I made it out okay. At least he was trying to stay quiet.

"Call it a bad habit. Now get ready." I crawled around them, to Francine's front bumper. I held up my fingers and counted down.

3, 2, 1

They went.

I leaned out around the bumper and aimed up the hill. I popped off two shots, enough for them to get an idea of where I was, then ducked back behind the tire.

The Jeep cracked and tinkled as bullets hit it. I was in the only really good cover I was gonna get until I managed to shake or bury these assholes, and I wasn't keen to leave. If I could sit here long enough, draw them to me, I might be able to get a clear shot and put 'em both down.

Not without its downsides. Shoot first and ask questions later doesn't work when you actually need answers, and I was starting to think I wouldn't mind knowing what all the violence was about. These two that were laying down fire on me were acting like professionals—they were staggering their shots, and they were shooting from two different positions, though I couldn't tell exactly where with the acoustics in that gully.

Then, the gunfire stopped.

I heard footfalls up the hill, through the earplugs and the ear pain, which meant they couldn't be very far away.

I risked a peek between the cars and saw a track suit in leather boots tumble down the hill to the other side of the car, and a pair of jeans run across from my right to circle around the front. Good coordination. No hesitation. They'd done this kind of work before.

Textbook two-man tactical moves. Careful covert explosives work. Just when my day couldn't get any better. That combination, you're looking at either ex-cop or ex-military, at least I hoped it was "ex." If they were current, then I'd just landed myself in a whole new circle of hell. So, just for fun, let's pretend it has to be "ex." That meant they were on the job, I'd stake my kidneys on it, and if I killed them, then as soon as Jerry and Lynn were back to civilization, whoever put out the contract would probably put another merc or two after my car crash buddies. Murder—good murder, anyway—doesn't come cheap, not when you've got professionals doing the deed. Someone willing to spend enough to get talent like this probably had enough cash on hand to bring in another team if this one failed.

This one was right on the other side of my engine block.

And moving.

If I stayed where I was, there were going to be at least two bodies on the ground, and if my count was right I had only about a one-third chance of not being one of them. Not my kind of odds.

And I could hear them splashing through the creek.

Nice thing about creek beds: all the rocks. The cock-eyed lay of the vehicles meant there was a little room underneath Francine. I laid down and slid underneath into the creek.

My whole body went shock-cold, and I had to fight to keep from gasping so loud I alerted them to my position. I managed it, though, laying face down, liquid nitrogen splashing down my belly and balls and holy fuck if I ever wind up stuck naked in Antarctica it won't be as cold as I was under that pile of metal.

The boots soft-pedaled along the side of Francine. I heard her doors open, one of the gunmen looking around inside her.

"Clear inside." The first voice was that kind of deep rasp that you expect in movie trailers, like some guy's throat had crawled out of a leather factory through the world's biggest ash tray.

"How bout the deal. Did they leave it?" The second guy sounded like he was younger, or at least less of a chain-smoker.

"Not in here, they didn't. Hmm...Looks like the guy shooting back was in here," Trailer-voice said. "Got some Hoppee's in the glove box. Trash on the passenger seat. Only one of 'em to worry about." Trailer-voice got out of Francine and moved around to the Jeep. He grunted and swore a little, and the Subaru above me shifted as his weight bore down on her front end as he climbed up and in. Then: "Not in here either."

"You sure?"

"Not like it's easy to hide. They must have taken it."

"Got a trail here." The younger guy paced downstream to behind the cars. "Looks like they went this way."

Francine shifted again. Trailer-voice's feet hit the water, and he stomped up onto the bank and measure-walked back to join younger-guy downstream. I kept trying to get myself turned around so I could kneecap them without blowing cover, but my shoulders wedged me down there. The only way out was sliding out sideways the way I came in.

So I made like a Zen master and contemplated the qualia of ice cubes until they decided what to do.

They conferred for a second. Low voices. Nothing I could make out. Then, the gunmen headed downstream at a jog.

I slid out and, staying right at the edge of visibility and stepping soft so they wouldn't hear me, and shivering like an electrocuted frog, I followed them.

THERE WASN'T A TRAIL DOWN there. All the walking meant picking my way through rocks and moss-covered fallen trees, and ferns, and the occasional skeleton from a dead cat, which I assumed was the result of a cougar having lunch rather than a witch trying to hex me, though I wouldn't have been surprised at the latter.

We were headed down hill, the three parties—Jerry and Lynn out front, leaving a trail that even a blind dog with no nose could find, followed by the hit men, who were moving as quick as they could without making noise or losing the trail, and me, leaving a blood trail of my own because I didn't have time to pull a first aid kit out of the car.

I was going to have to do something about that. It would take me a while to bleed out, but between all the adrenaline and the cold I was gonna be in miserable shape if I lost enough blood to notice. And my shirt was already soaked with it.

If I did anything about it now, they were going to hear me. I couldn't even think about that arm being part of my body or I was going to wince and yowl loud enough that every coyote in the neighborhood would think it was orgy time.

Knowing what was up ahead—which I didn't—I might have been able to circle around and lay a clever trap. Ambush them. As it was, I was hard pressed to keep up with them. The two of them had experience moving over ground like this, as a team, whereas I wasn't exactly up to snuff on my outdoorsman's merit badge.

We passed next to a vertical retaining wall holding up the road. Couldn't quite see the guard rail through the fog but I could see the glow of headlights from the sparse commuter traffic heading east and up, and I realized I was going to have to either shoot the mercs now or give up the chase, go back to the car and fix the holes in my arm, and then try to run them down before they found Jerry and Lynn and redecorated their faces with red-and-black polka dots.

The fog was thicker down here. After I got to the other side of the bridge I only had about twenty feet of visibility. I had to take my earplugs out, stick them in my pocket, so I could follow by sound.

I heard splashing in the creek, and a voice exchange I couldn't make out. Maybe the trail crossed to the other side, and they were following it. I kept my eyes peeled for the first likely crossing where I wouldn't have to splash in the stream, and didn't find a hell of a lot.

No stepping stones. Dammit.

Wound up wading through, quiet as I could. Soft steps, slow moves. About fifteen feet across and a good foot deep in the channel. The stream was getting faster, probably fed by little springs I'd overlooked as damp patches in the ground, maybe runoff from the condensation on the road.

The footprints on the other side weren't hard to find. Half-soaked mud's better than ink for leaving a good foot trail. I followed on, trying like hell to catch up to within ear-shot.

The cold was bone-deep now, but I wasn't light-headed, so it had to be the water, not the blood loss.

What you need right now, Lantham, is a good wing man. Where the fuck is Rachael?

She was always good in a tight corner. It doesn't get much tighter than this. Having her around right now would seriously save my bacon.

Even if it didn't, at least I wouldn't have to die alone in the middle of the woods.

The sides of the gully steepened on the other side, carved by the creek which ran against sheer walls. I hunched down, crept along the ground so I could spot the footprints easier. Not easy once we got away from the mud at the creek's edge. I never got trained in hunting and tracking, so looking for anything that might be man spoor slowed me down to a crawl.

A narrow game trail climbed up the south side of the gully. The ground was covered with forest carpet—redwood leavings and pine needles and other leaves—so footprints were out. But the carpet had scuffs that looked recent, and there were some broken branches sticking out from the side, as if someone had gotten their jacket hooked on a low-hanging oak limb.

I didn't have anything else to go buy, so I laid my money that everyone had followed the path so they wouldn't have to deal with the water and rocks in the creek bed.

Dammit, Lynn, I told you to head straight downstream. How was I supposed to find them if they went off plan?

Didn't help that I had to trust the judgment of the contractors. I had to assume that, given their qualifications, they could track better than I could. Besides, if Lynn and Jerry managed to evade the gun-toting loonies on their tail (I include myself in this calculus—I may be an idiot, I am at least a self-aware idiot), at least I wouldn't have to worry about them. I could track them down and get their insurance information tomorrow. I figured I knew where their wrecked car was—it's not like I'd have trouble finding them once this little impromptu action movie ground to a hopefully-anticlimactic end.

I was about a hundred feet above the creek now, on a little trail that had no reason to exist, as far as I could tell. Maybe it was the front stairway for the singles bar serving the local deer population. But the further I got up the hill, the less forest carpet I was walking over.

Dry dirt. Faint footprints. And eventually, as the ground got rockier, no footprints. And me, in the middle of a cotton-candy cloud like some rube with a social media startup.

For the next hundred yards, the trail held.

Then it forked. And you know where that left me?

I'll give you a hint: it sounds like "forked."

One trail moved right and continued on a level. The left one kept climbing into the forest. Neither one of them had any prints I could spot, and nothing else that might tell me which way the parade passed. No blood trails—so I was probably the only one bleeding—no twigs laying across the path that looked freshly broken, nothing else that looked obvious to my under-trained eyes.

That's the other thing about Rachael's whole disappearing act that I haven't gotten used to yet. She could track an elk over a granite bluff in the dark using only her fingers, or at least that's what Cal tells me. Even considering it might be a proud papa's boast, the fact that she had his respect in that department means she knows her shit where wilderness work was concerned.

And she wasn't here. I decided that if I could stay alive (and not get any civilians killed) long enough to actually kill Rachael, I could count that a solid win, something worth putting on my tombstone. *Here lies Clarke Lantham. Shitty cop, decent PI, achieved greatness by assassinating a blue-haired goth punk half his age.*

Okay, not quite half my age, but if anyone's ever made me feel older, I can't remember it on account of the dementia.

I could hear the road somewhere below me, off on the far side of the ravine. Hadn't realized I'd climbed so far. I'd had signal on the road. Time to call in some backup.

"Cal, don't fail me now." I pulled out my trusty phone, my one true friend, the cybernetic extension of my brain that I'd loaded up with my custom snooperino software suite, and swiped the screen to wake it up.

Only to find out that it was in a coma.

The creek, you moron. I'd been laying face down in the creek, with that phone in my front pocket, taking a bath along with the rest of me. And the damn thing had drowned.

Next time, waterproof case. Fat lot of good that did me now.

But if I could get back up to the road, maybe I could flag someone down.

It would mean leaving the chickens to the wolves, but if I could get access to a cell phone, I would be able to get the sheriff's department down here.

But the hour it would take to get the cops on scene, plus the hours it would take to find anyone in this forest? That's the better part of the day before I could be sure the civvies were safe. That amounts to pulling the trigger myself.

If I'm gonna pull a trigger, I'd rather do it in person. Call it a character flaw.

But as long as I was standing at that fork in the trail, I figured I'd better do what I could to bandage my arm. I stripped out of my jacket. Bits of it had worked into the shredded meat I called a tricep, so peeling it off felt like I was trying to evict a fishing hook colony the hard way.

I did manage not to yowl. The opiates your body produces when you're in shock are the best drugs on the fucking planet—and if I wasn't in shock at that point, I didn't have any business knowing the word.

The leather was soaked in blood from above my elbow

to the cuff, which had absorbed enough of the tacky stuff to feel like it had been dipped in paraffin and left to cool. The point of impact was punctured with four holes, all buckshot. I was damn lucky they'd only winged me—another eight or ten inches to the right and they'd have ventilated my lungs from the back.

I leaned, back against a convenient bay tree, on the grounds that if I was going to look like I'd dipped my arm in spaghetti sauce I might as well smell like it, too. With a good prop, I didn't have to worry about pitching forward down the hill. Good thing I did, cause when I touched the raw meat hanging out of my arm I just about passed out.

This is not how a good gunshot wound feels. The fact that I can use the phrase "good gunshot wound" with a straight face probably proves all the snarky comments Rachael ever made about my IQ, and legitimizes all the fretting Nya does over me, but I won't tell them if you don't.

At least the blood was well tacky and not flowing too much. A little pressure and it should seal right up, then I could worry about getting the lead taken out later.

Only thing I had for a bandage was my shirt. It was cold in that fog bank. But I didn't see as how I had much choice. I tore it off—it hurt less than taking it off properly—and folded it for a bandage, then bit down on one end and looped the other around my bicep. Tied it off, not tight enough to cut off the circulation, but tight enough to make all my nerve endings crawl under the bed and start whimpering.

I swallowed hard, kept a hold on my stomach and my

equilibrium. I must've looked like hell. Cold sweat. Clammy skin. Half-collapsed against a gnarled tree trunk. Freezing from the soaking I got all down my front. Not a whole hell of a lot of interest in doing anything but settling down for a good coma.

Goddammit, Lantham, if you don't get back on your feet, you'll never be able to look Erica in the eye again.

One of the disadvantages of dating a Fed: you gotta keep your cop bona fides all polished and shiny. If her people found me dead or comatose out here, and two civilians with lead-flavored heart implants just down the hill, she'd never live it down. There goes Agent Ellis, the one that used to sleep with that loser PI. Now I ask you, what kind of man does that to a woman he claims to love?

Push off the tree. Make the wager that the civvies would follow the creek, cause some ogre with a gun told them to. Take the right fork, cause it might just snake back down. Plow forward like someone's life depends on it, cause it probably does.

Remember to breathe.

Don't hyperventilate.

Sometimes, keeping those two things in balance constitutes a good day, you know?

Feet on the ground. Roots across the path. Moss.

The ground, softer again. Down here where the water hangs out.

I could hear the creek below me. Couldn't be more than another twenty yards.

There were prints in the mud, a lot of prints. Like

people used this trail a lot. There must be a house around here somewhere. My head settled down a little bit, I could think straight. I could move faster, too.

The fog was thinning. I could see maybe a hundred feet now. The other side of the creek bed wasn't as sheer as it used to be, but it wasn't exactly a picnic-worthy park slope. Enough that I could spot moving shadows below and ahead. Couldn't tell if they were animals or people. I knew they couldn't be plants moving in the wind, cause there wasn't any wind.

Perfect acoustics for sound to crawl up the hill to me.

"Missed 'em, I'm telling you."

"Where?"

"Back up at the fork."

"Not possible, you saw the thread."

False lead. Brockman said he did search and rescue in his Navy days. He planted it.

"Sold."

And the shadows turned around. If I could see them, they'd be able to see me as soon as I moved, if not sooner.

The trail below me doubled back about eight yards in front of me, snaking down to the pebble-strewn stream bed almost directly below me, out of sight behind a redwood stand. I played statue until they were behind the trees, then took off uphill at a run—or as close to one as I could manage—until I made it back up to that bay tree.

It had a tangle of rocks and roots underneath it. I took a leap up onto the rocks, slung myself around the back, laid sidelong against it and hoped to hell I didn't leave any footprints that would attract their notice. And that I was skinny enough to escape notice behind that trunk. It was almost three feet across, and I was dressed in neutral colors—thank God for good tactical habits.

They came jogging up the trail, turned, headed toward the uphill fork. I held my breath. They blew right by like a stiff canyon breeze. I'd wanted them where I could get some answers, now I had them.

For a few seconds, I actually considered taking them down right there. I was behind them, I had the drop on them. Chances were good I could knock at least one of them off before they could return fire. Maybe both of them.

But that meant trusting my luck against two men with a lot more stalk-and-kill training than I had, or shooting them both in the back and hoping I got one-shot-kills. It meant giving up on finding out who sent them, and it meant maybe not finding Lynn and Jerry again. They were city folk. Granted that we weren't far from civilization, but people have died less than a hundred yards from the road because they broke a leg or got so disoriented they didn't know which way was up.

I was going to have to bide my time.

I waited until they were up around the next bend.

Hook my right around the trunk, swing out. Take a couple quick steps down to the path. Land in a crouch. Quiet as birds gliding through the too-thick air.

Move along, fast as I can. Stay low. Keep them just barely in sight.

They weren't worrying about being subtle, not yet.

They walked tall and careful, the kind of steady pace that takes forever until you realize it's chewing up the miles without thinking, like a bulldozer in low gear.

This plan was only going to play well until I screwed up and attracted their attention, or they happened on their quarry. Then it was all shooting, all the time, and that's if things went down well. Don't get me wrong, I don't mind shooting someone when shooting is what they need, but it's not something I do for entertainment. There's too much paperwork, for one thing. And for another, you always risk hitting the stray civilian on the far side of your target.

The ground in front of me was getting stony. Rock outcroppings sticking out from the erosion channel. Granite and shale, good bedrock stuff. Some of them small enough that they might be useful.

The gunmen were stopped a little way ahead again. The taller one was half crouched, studying something on the ground. They were arguing over something, doing it quiet enough that I couldn't hear. I took the chance to squat down, grab a stone with my left. I gripped, tested the weight. My fingers worked well enough that I could hang onto it, so I probably didn't have any ligament damage.

Hurt like hell, though, and it didn't weigh much. Figured it was worth it if it came in handy. Throwing something at the bad guys buys you an extra second, sometimes, if you throw it at their face. Makes 'em flinch. Even a pillow will do in a pinch.

But rocks are better, especially if you score a hit.

They moved again. Still further along the path. If I was them, I'd be wondering where the hell those two civvies went—and I'll bet my left nut that's what they were arguing about.

The path curved around to the left around a granite finger.

They quick-footed around it—I followed as far as the rock. Stopped before ducking around. Listened as hard as I could. Couldn't hear anything on the other side.

I could hear something, though. Something weird.

A whippoorwill. We don't have whippoorwills around the Bay. Hopefully the bad guys don't know that. Only reason I've ever heard one is because I watch TV, and there was an episode of Lassie I saw on reruns once where Timmy was learning bird calls.

Checked the sound. Just above me and to my left.

Lynn's slick-black hair poked out from the top of the rock outcrop. Smart woman. I nodded to her, looked for a way to scramble up. It meant I had to holster my weapon, not something that makes a Lantham all kinds of happy.

Handgun in the holster. Rock in the jacket pocket. It fit, but barely.

Climbing one-handed? Also not my favorite activity. But I managed. Even managed without knocking anything loose and making any noise. There was a highway up the rock face—easy progression of handholds and footholds, for those of you who haven't trusted your life to chalk-and-granite supporting you forty feet up a sheer rock wall—not obvious from the bottom, but once you got the first few steps up you could see it easy. Couldn't have been better if someone laid a peg trail. I even managed it one-handed.

Up top, the finger was flat. It retreated into the soft hillside and under the trees. Looked like another trail up here, too. Jerry sat up by the trees, babying his left knee. He was bleeding, but not much. Probably skinned it scrambling up over the edge—couldn't blame him, there weren't a lot of good hand-holds at the top, and I had a hell of a time getting up myself without giving up and using the hillside, which would have knocked stones and dirt loose and given the game away.

That was to my left. To my right, and not very far to my right, I saw Lynn crouched frog-fashion on the edge, watching the trail, keeping low. I couldn't tell yet whether she actually saw anybody or whether she was just making sure the bad guys didn't double back.

I got low and crept up near her. Pulled my earplugs, closed my eyes, listened. I could hear them down there, not very far off. More suppressed whispers. If we actually moved around much up here we'd give the game away.

Well, there was one way to deal with that. I leaned toward Lynn and barely-whispered "How far can you throw?"

"What?"

I showed her the rock in my pocket. In fairness, I *was* happy to see her. Happy to see them both. Nice to not have them dead, you know?

"Can you throw? Far enough to hit the far side?"

She nodded, but she looked like she thought I was insane. I didn't have time to disabuse her of that notion, and I'd lost too much blood to lie convincingly anyway.

"Is Jerry good to move?"

"Think so."

"Good." I nodded into the fog filling the ravine. "Do it."

She gave that rock a good solid fling, and about two seconds later we herd it clop against a tree on the other side, then thunk-snap-smack-skitter down the hillside to the creek bed.

It was answered by footfalls, and skitters. Our two stalkers were going down the hillside as quick as they could. They'd assume they mistook the trail, find a way up the other side of the creek. Depending on what the terrain was like, we'd just bought anywhere between ten minutes and an hour. Plenty of time to get the hell out of here.

"Okay, that's it. Get him. Go. Up the trail." I stayed behind a couple minutes and listened, just to make sure the deception took. I didn't hear anything I wasn't expecting. The men splashed through the creek. That put them at least three minutes away, even at top speed and in excellent condition, which I assumed they had to be.

Lynn and Jerry were taking the trail up from the cliff, didn't take me long to catch up. By the time I did, I was pretty sure we were heading up into either a park or into someone's back yard.

"Hold on, hold on, this could be exactly what we need." I took point. Kept about five yards ahead, just enough to see around corners. I had them stay in the middle of the path. Less chance of them stepping on a twig and turning this whole thing into a raging cliché.

I hate clichés. At least, when they don't happen where they're supposed to, on screen, to actors. Anything that happens to actors, I'm okay with. I dated one in college. You learn great life lessons that way—like "don't."

Pavement, over the next rise. Well, not pavement so much as cinderblocks laid into the earth, with manicured grass growing up through the holes. Definitely someone's yard. The paving led up a gentle grade, swooped left around a stand of redwoods, and ended at a building.

I peeked around the redwoods.

Definitely a house. Empty, too, by the looks of it. A hunting cabin, or a summer house, and the owner wasn't in town.

A peek in the windows told me it was probably empty, but there might have been someone napping inside.

I flagged the two commuters up to the house.

"Jerry," I said when they got alongside, "check the garage. I'll knock on the door. Make sure nobody's home."

"And if they aren't?"

"It's a surprise."

9:40 AM, THURSDAY

SINCE MINE WERE STASHED IN one of Francine's secret hidey-holes, I had to improvise a lock pick. I didn't have a lot to work with. Wound up using a pocket knife, figured I'd better pray they didn't have an alarm system installed. People who buy out in this area tend to have more money than sense—they pretty much have more money than about ninety nine percent of the people on the planet—and you can count on people like that to put alarms on everything.

Then again, a good alarm service might get the cops here sooner rather than later. I'd have some fancy footwork on the breaking-and-entering charge, but we'd at least get some more guns on the ground, and on the right side. I figured, either way, there wasn't much point in standing on ceremony when I could stomp on it instead.

Bathroom windows are the easiest. Too small for most people to worry about, and almost nobody alarms them. I popped its screen off, jimmied the window open with that trusty little buck knife. I got through by limping my dead-ish arm in first, breathing all the way out to collapse my rib cage, then squirming. Go through at enough of an angle, you can collapse your shoulders like a cat squeezing under your bedroom door to torment the dog that's sleeping next to you on the bed.

That cat's been a pain in my sphincter since it moved in with its mistress over a year ago. The things I put up with to make Nya happy.

But I digress. Where was I?

Oh, right. Felonies. B&Es. Yeah, the things you learn in this kind of work could fill a few books, the kind your mother wouldn't want you to read. Neither would your lawyer, for that matter.

The absent owners did have an alarm system. An older one. Found the keypad in the entryway. Also found the green light on, because they forgot to arm it when they left. That was about a month ago, maybe two, judging by the dust.

"WELL, BOYS AND GIRLS," the fact that there was only one of each didn't slow me down. Now that I'd had a good long drink of water—and paid the rent on this morning's coffee—the time had come to do some actual work, "we don't have a lot of time. Who's got a phone?"

Lynn shook her head. "I'm afraid I was using it when we crashed. I dropped it in the car."

"Jerry, you were trying to call out..."

"Um..." Jerry patted his pockets, then closed his eyes. A look came over his face that said the whole next sentence before he opened his mouth. "I...um...it must've fallen out."

That would be what they picked up off the trail. So

they have it now. "Okay, we'll use the house line. We've got a few minutes, if we're lucky, before they find this place and figure out we're in here. We're not gonna stick around long, but while we're here, there are some rules. Nobody goes near the windows. In fact, nobody goes into a room where the blinds or the drapes aren't closed." I pointed at the windows in here—I'd pulled the gauze drapes on the way through. Nobody outside would be able to see in. "Nobody turns a light on, nobody talks louder than a I'm talking now." I was speaking quietly enough that they wouldn't have been able to hear me if I wasn't sitting on a chair across from the two of them on the rough-weave tweed sofa. "You understand this?"

"Yes," Jerry said.

Lynn merely nodded.

"Okay, sit tight for a second. Don't move." I got up, looked around for a phone, didn't find one. Not in the bathroom, the kitchen, the living room, the master bedroom.

What kind of asshole has a mountain cabin with no phone? The kind that has wireless everything, that's what kind. Goddammit.

"Right, so, no cavalry yet," I said when I gave up and got back to the living room, "so we're gonna have to fend for ourselves. If you want me to keep you both alive, I need a few things from you. Answers, for one. Background. And some creativity."

The two of them shifted uncomfortably, like I was their parent and just about to ask the question that would make them both lie about hosting the house party where their high school's quarterback ruined my priceless antique ship-in-a-bottle by using it as an enema bag.

"One at a time, then. Lynn, you start. Who's Palmer?"

"Our business partner," she folded her arms over her chest, crossed her legs. This was not a subject she wanted me prying into.

"And that business is..."

"None of yours."

So she was one of those. Oh, joy. "Your call. I'll get my ass to a hospital and you fine people will hear from me once I'm all patched up. For the accident—assuming you survive the afternoon. I'll need your driver's licenses, insurance info, that kind of stuff."

"Hey...hey now," Jerry stuttered—all this time I'd thought it was the stress, but I'd read him wrong. Dude really did have a stutter, which narrowed the kind of business he must be in, or at least the job he had in it, by a good bit. "You can't...can't j...just leave us here."

I stood back up. These two were from the Valley, I figured they wouldn't buy a walk-out unless I actually walked out. But once they bought it, they'd fold like used Kleenex. "You'll be fine. If you look around here you might find a shotgun or something—people sometimes keep them in places like this. Course, there might not be any ammo, but if you point it and look convincing, you might not have to actually pull the trigger."

"Where do you think you're going?" Lynn was obviously the kind of woman who was used to getting what she wanted, and used to people doing as she told them. She had the kind of careful-speech pattern that you find in upper-class Pennsylvanians and second-generation Koreans. Figured her for the CEO of whatever company these guys were involved in. She had the bearing. And the entitlement. That kind of thing can get you a long way in the Valley, if you can back it up. Doesn't get you so much as a raw chicken wing with me.

"You're the ones whose car they wired. The two of you—or at least, one of you—is who they want dead. I'm leaving the blast radius before that grenade goes off. Cheers." I got my hand on the front doorknob.

Turned it.

"Wait." Lynn. "You say you are a private detective. What do you charge?"

"Well, that depends. What am I getting into?"

The two of them looked at each other. Jerry inclined his head. Lynn shrugged.

"Okay, start from the beginning," I said. "Who are the two of you, besides 'Jerry' and 'Lynn,'"

"Lynnette Park. CEO of Personae."

"Haven't heard of that one."

"We're a blockchain-based identity brokerage."

"Right." Note to self: read up on blockchain. As far as I knew it had something to do with Bitcoin and all its friends. "And you?"

"G...G...Gerald Manders. I'm the brains of the outfit."

"He's our CTO. He developed the implementation."

"So if I have a spare identity, I talk to you, and you sell it for Bitcoins?"

That, at least, got a smile. Smiling makes tongues wag a little looser, makes people more willing to go places they might not want to.

"So who's Palmer?"

"Palmer Shara," she said. "The CFO. One third partner. He has plans for us. Big plans."

"What kind of big?"

"Eight figures. Maybe nine."

"Wowzers." Sometimes, you gotta break out the Inspector Gadget.

"So why did he plant a bomb in your car?"

"Well...I don't know it was him. It's just..."

"When I asked if you'd pissed anyone off lately, you said 'not yet.'"

"That's right."

"Define 'yet'."

"There's a pitch session this afternoon. Then we vote on Palmer's deal."

"We...we are...g...g...going to turn it down."

"And you think he's willing to kill you for that?" People have killed for less, but the Valley's particular brand of cutthroat doesn't usually involve actual cutting of actual throats. People around here tend to be...well, not subtle, exactly, but they love good PR, and dead bodies tend to fuck with that. Let me put it this way: In Japan, business is war. In the Valley, it's a game. People can die in football as well as in a battle, but on the battlefield, the killing is the point. In football, you kill someone, you lose yardage. "Not really page one of the lean startup playbook. Last time anyone around here got really whacked was when that guy spiked the office punchbowl with acid at Facebook's Christmas party." Well, that and

Hans Reiser's wife, but that was personal, not business.

"Maybe..." Lynn chewed on her bottom lip. From my extremely limited exposure to her mannerisms, she didn't strike me as the fretful type. Scheming, maybe. Iron-nerved, for sure. But she was coming over worried. The kind of worried that makes mothers drown their kids to save them from the apocalypse. Gunfire hadn't made her worry this much.

"What is it?" Then I got it. "Who was the offer from?"

"That's the th...th...thing," Jerry said. "He wouldn't say. They just wanted to b...buy us out. Eighty million, cash. No questions asked."

"We don't even have our public beta till next Tuesday," Lynn came in right on top of him.

"And you sell...what?"

"Jerry." She sounded bored.

"Our patent. It's a method for establishing trust in online transactions between anonymous parties—reputation maintenance, escrow, everything you might want—without having to ever give up your name or IP."

"So we're talking, what? Someone wants to bury the tech?"

"That's what we think, yeah."

"So why kill you? Don't tell me this Palmer guy inherits." The last thing I needed was to get involved in a tech-world tontine.

"Not my stock. Jerry?"

Jerry shook his head. "My wife get...s...s everything."

"And would your heirs vote with Palmer if you died?"

Lynn seemed to go on a journey inside herself, like she was checking every corner of her mind. It didn't take her long. "No. My stock would go into trust for my daughters, and the executor—my husband—knows the situation."

"So nothing then...wait a minute." I love that moment when a couple pieces fit into place. Makes me feel like I might not be quite as insane as the voices say I am. "You think the buyer...no...dammit. Same problem. Unless they just want to pooch the beta." I could think of about a dozen parties who'd give their left nut to keep this thing off the market, and another dozen who'd be happy to do the same thing to make sure it got to market. If these guys had any press at all, even in venture circles, they'd have eyes on them for everyone from intelligence services to foreign mobs to...oh, I really didn't like where this was going. "Why were the two of you driving into Mountain View? Don't tell me you live out there and commute together."

"No. We're in Richmond. We just had a meeting this morning."

"Who takes a meeting at six in the morning in Pescadero?"

Lynn shook her head. "It's not important."

"Whoever rigged your car followed you from that meeting." I hate playing connect-the-dots for civilians. Feels like one step above stealing a kindergartener's coloring book because he thinks the crayons are food. "They knew how to find you. So either they've got a tail on you, or they knew you'd be there, or the meeting was bait."

"M...m...maybe we oughta tell him."

"Fine. Whatever. Right. We were out at a campground by Pescadero to see this fellow, Ferris. A friend of ours referred him. He's a consultant of some kind..."

"Wait. Ferris. Gus Ferris. At Camp Loma Mar?"

"Um...yeah."

"Oh, this can't be good."

"What?"

"Nothing. Long story, not important." I needed to get back to that car. If Ferris was mixed up in this, whatever was in that envelope Cal gave me might mark me out for a target, too. "Look, we've got to get out of here now. Jerry, is there anything in the garage?"

He shook his head. "Didn't l...look like it."

"Okay. Then we've gotta go out the hard way. Lynne, give me your card."

"What?"

"Your business card. You have some on you, right?"

She dug in her pocket, produced a little silver card holder. She handed a card over to me.

"Great. I'll call you tonight, assuming we all survive this. Job like this, I get five hundred bucks plus medical bills. One last thing."

"W...what's th...that?"

"Back at the car—they were looking for something. They said it wasn't the kind of thing that was easy to hide. Any idea what it was?"

They both looked at me blankly. Maybe they weren't carrying anything? Maybe it was all about the envelope

Cal gave me?

So why did they bomb the Jeep's brakes, then?

"Fine." I wasn't exactly flush with time. "I'll ask again when I call tonight. I consider this," I tapped the bandage on my arm, "A blood contract, and trust me, you don't want to be on my bad side. The driveway of this place has to land on the main road. I want the two of you to get out and head for the highway. Flag someone down. Anyone. Get their phone. Call the cops, get the hell out of here."

"Where are you going?"

"I'm going to make sure that nobody follows you."

10:30 AM, THURSDAY

I WOULDN'T FIND OUT ABOUT it till later, but Nya was going crazy back at the office. When she couldn't raise me about a client call that came in—one of my insurance clients, so not somebody we wanted to keep waiting—she tried turning on my cell phone locater to figure out where I'd gotten to. When that didn't work, she started working her way down the list of frequent contacts to see if I'd turned up anywhere.

Shoulda left a note. Normally I would, but I was preoccupied this morning, and besides, I had my phone, then, and you're never out of touch when you're wearing a phone. Unless you have to hide from gunmen in a creek.

But, walking back down that trail, I knew she had to be going nuts by now. Nya does that. One of the things that makes her a hell of an assistant. She can hold down a fort like nobody's business, and she's got razor-sharp instincts where people are concerned. Part of what makes her special. Might sound silly under the circumstances, but I was feeling more than a little guilty about putting her through that kind of worry. She already had enough where Rachael was concerned.

On the other hand, if I'd been home this morning, I'd have woken up to Nya cooking me breakfast, which is always a delicate diplomatic undertaking.

Well, with a little luck I'd put an end to her misery. Assuming I could get back to the cars, and without getting shot. Between here and there, I needed to do a little hunting. If those two mercs really had staked out Lynn and Jerry, and followed them back from the meet with Cal's friend out in Pescadero, then either whoever was on their tail wanted them to disappear *after* they had that meeting. Or they were improvising after their original plan got derailed by the CEO and the CTO going AWOL this early in the AM.

Or Gus Ferris, who Cal hired me to make a delivery to, was behind the whole thing. What was it Cal had said?

Don't get pulled over while you're carrying this.

Or something like that.

So what was it that Cal had me carrying? I'd never made the delivery. It was still in the car.

It is still in the car.

Were they looking for the package Cal gave me?

If these bastards were after people who'd just met with Ferris, were they also interested in someone who was about to meet with him? Was Ferris the reason Jerry and Lynn were targets, or was that a coincidence?

I needed to see what was in that file. Under the circumstances, I figured Cal wouldn't begrudge me that. If seeing it painted a target on my back, well, it was just gonna have to jockey for space with the ten other targets I figured I'd collected over the years.

Kinda puts an expiration date on the detective agency. Living to a hundred would be nice, but I've always figured I'd check out before sixty. A bullet or a car crash, probably, and I've got my money on the bullet. They seem to like me a little bit too much for my own good.

Fast progress back to the crash site wasn't in the cards. Had to watch my step. Couldn't make any noise. To be perfectly honest, I was kinda shocked they hadn't caught up with us at the house. Not that we'd stayed there long, but it was long enough. I wondered how far down that false trail they went before they gave up and doubled back to figure out where they lost us. They had to know by now they'd chased a false lead.

Those two worried me, and not because they hadn't picked up my scent yet. It's no small thing to send professionals to kill a couple entrepreneurs. I've been around enough professionals in the last couple years to get something through my head, something you don't get from action movies, something that told me a lot more at the back of this than I really wanted to know about:

You don't just hire mercs cause you have a lot of money and you want to make sure a job gets done good and permanent. You hire mercs, and send 'em in with guns lighting up like crazy, when you don't care who knows it was a murder.

Not just a murder, but a hit.

There was no attempt to deflect blame here. There wasn't anything approaching subtlety. Anyone who looked at that brake cylinder would spot that it was a bomb. Anyone who looked at that accident scene would find spent brass all around. Anyone who found the bodies wouldn't be able to miss the gunshot wounds. And there was no prayer that an accident would go undiscovered this close to a major road (or what passed for one out here) lined with rich-folks retreats, campgrounds, conference centers, and state parks.

Whoever did this didn't *care* if the cops knew there was a major hit here. They couldn't give a shit. Which meant that either they considered themselves untouchable, or...

Or they were sending a message.

But to who?

And, for that matter, what did the message actually say?

Don't fuck with us. That's what it said. That, or something like it.

I tried to stay out of the creek bed, much as I could, but it was slow going over the trails, and I was leaving footprints, and if I did come across the goon squad I wasn't going to have a lot of tactical options, especially with one arm more-or-less out of service and the rest of me freezing in the fog.

No shirt, no sleeve? No shit. Glad I had my shoes. If I kept my jacket zipped up I could technically still go into a grocery store.

The fog wasn't burning off. It had thinned a bit, but that's about all it looked like it was going to give today. Maybe there was low overcast on the coast and I was just socked in at the wrong altitude, maybe there was some kind of warm current welling up from the continental shelf. Whatever it was, it meant I got to wade through something that wasn't quite air and wasn't quite a swimming pool, and shivering from the cold soak that would never dry out, and wondering why I hadn't just given up and grown gills before I was born. I'd have done better as a fish. I'm too ugly for a shark to eat, and there are a lot of gorgeous reefs in the world where I'd be happy to spend my life scuba diving with my own built-in tanks.

Wouldn't have to worry about gunmen that way. Or bloody-minded tweeny women and their friend-abandoning ways. I'd have given anything to have Rachael there in that ravine with me just then. Two years ago, I'd never have believed it if you'd told me that I'd prefer working with a partner to without, but anything you told that bitter asshole would've gotten you a sneer. Now that I'm all civilized and domesticated, this lone wolf bit is getting tired.

Doubly so when I step around the corner and just about run into the very creeps I'm stalking.

They didn't see me right off. They were crouched on the ground, like they were trying to decode some footprints. Figure out where they'd gone wrong. Gave me a chance to duck back around the corner and consider my options.

Okay, Lantham. You could just walk right by them. They haven't seen you yet. Don't know you're here.

Right, except we had traded shots.

Through the fog, numbskull. They don't know who was shooting at them.

Which was true, except I did have this big bloody wound in my arm.

It's hidden under a jacket.

Which is shredded.

It's black leather and you can only see the shred from the back of the one arm.

Except my entire left arm is covered in blood and I'm not wearing a shirt.

So pull the backup weapon, stick it in your pocket with your left hand. They won't see the blood if they don't see skin, then you've got a handy backup.

I'd need to pass them on the left, but I could make that work if I jogged back along the creek bed a little bit, crossed to the far side, and came strolling back up like I was any other hiker. People hike by creeks, right? I could be a local writer out looking for inspiration. A naturalist hunting some rare species of spotted salamander.

I remembered to stick my earplugs back in.

I strolled around that bend like I owned the place, and these two almost jumped up and rounded on me. The fog set my visibility at about forty feet, but I pretended not to notice them until they were about five yards off—you know, like normal people do.

My first good look at the two of them. They both dressed to disappear. Jeans. Colombia windbreakers. Doc Martins. Clean-shaven. Late 20s, early thirties. Both male—after hearing their voices earlier, I'd have been slightly terrified if one of them turned out to be a woman—both just under six feet. Mixed race of some sort, not too dark, not too white. Nothing whatsoever to stick in the memory. A pair of guys like this that could walk through any neighborhood in the whole country and not ever get the slightest notice. Like they got selected from the "Generic dudes" section of the Sears catalog.

I gave them a little wave.

"Mornin'," I said. "Gorgeous day. You guys tickling?"

That set them both looking at each other like I was speaking Latin or something. Not classical scholars then. *Quod erat demonstrandum.*

"What?" They didn't look exactly alike. This guy was smaller, and had the ash-tray-leather voice. Narrowish shoulders, red trim on the windbreaker.

"Trout tickling. Hand fishing. You know, when you...ah, never mind. Lose something in the water?"

The bigger one—Papa Smurf, I figured, for the blue trim and the linebacker shoulders—smiled a quick smile, and not the kind of smile that makes you want to order him a drink. "Deer hunting. Got a trail."

I decided not to point out that they didn't have rifles and weren't wearing orange. I knew one of them was packing a nine and the other had a shotgun, but I couldn't see the armaments, which meant they'd stowed 'em for some reason. Maybe so that innocent passers-by like yours truly wouldn't get all freaky on them.

"Good luck." I tried to walk on past. Thought for a moment about getting the drop on them, but I couldn't think of any way that scenario played out that didn't leave bodies on the deck. I could only think of a handful where there was one dead body and it wasn't mine. I figured it was better to split them up, get one out of commission, and then worry about the guy still standing.

Just had to get past them without them taking an interest.

"Hey!" Trailer-voice. I'd only gotten a few steps past the two of them. "You haven't seen anyone down that way, have you? We, uh, we don't want to shoot anyone if we miss a deer."

I kept walking. Twirled on my heels, walked backwards. They were both facing me. Couldn't tell if it was because they were sizing me up, or hiding their guns,or just good tactical practice of never turning your back on a threat.

God, I hoped I didn't ping as "threat" on their radar.

"Not a one." *I'd better go for folksy. Folksy works. Friendly, non-threatening. The kind of person who isn't worth pulling a gun on.* "Nice peaceful morning. Good luck. I'll try to scare any deer I see down this way."

Nothing here to see, guys, just an everyday mountain dude walking along with his hands in his pockets.

First thing you learn as a cop: never turn your back on guys with guns. Except, if I didn't, they were gonna make me and plug me.

And if I did, and I read them wrong, they'd plug me in the back.

And I had my earplugs in, so I couldn't listen for them pulling a weapon.

Thinking through all this took about a quarter second—not long enough to disturb anyone.

I took my right hand, the one that wasn't covered in

dried blood, and brushed it back past my ear, like I was scratching an itch. Plucked out the plug. Palmed it. Nodded to the two mercs like they were just regular guys out for a fog-light walk by the creek.

They nodded back. Nice smiles. Aligator smiles.

Turn around now, Lantham, or you're deader than Lincoln.

Lincoln got shot in the back, too.

To more steps. I heard them move.

Squeezed the grip on the .357 in my pocket.

Then, splashing in the creek. Light splashing.

Heading the other way.

They were checking downstream.

They'd lost interest in me.

Well thank fuck for that.

I kept on as steady a stride as I could manage. Nice relaxed pace. The kind of pace you make when you're just out for a stroll on a foggy morning. Trust the long legs to eat up the distance fast enough to be around the bend before they reconsidered.

Before one of them decided to wonder why I'd kept my left hand in my pocket like that.

But I couldn't hear anything. And when the ravine snaked around to the left again, and the water got wider and the banks got narrower, they weren't following me.

I jogged forward so I could get some kind of vantage. Watch the valley behind me. Try to check to make sure they weren't following me.

On the far side, a little ways up the hill, with the most unobstructed view down around the bend, I found a tree I could hunker behind.

The fog was thinner than it had been just ten minutes earlier. Might be burning off for good. Right now I couldn't decide if that would me an advantage or not.

For the moment, though, it wasn't a bad thing. I could see all the way down to the next bend, well past where I'd left those two sloshing around in the creek.

Right then, leaning against that moss-covered bay bark, I let out a breath I didn't know I'd been holding. Enough breath to inflate a blimp five times over.

Then I had to remember how to breathe again. I still had maybe half a mile to go upstream before I got to the wrecks.

Time to get moving.

10:50 AM, THURSDAY

FOUND FRANCINE JUST WHERE I left her. Cal's manila envelope, too, still in the underdash sash—he'd told me not to get caught with it. I didn't want it sitting in plain sight if I got pulled over for speeding.

I didn't want to advertise my presence, so I folded the seats down in the back and laid under the blanket while I checked it out. To anyone walking by, I was just another lump in the cargo.

The envelope had two words on it:

Requested Material

The thing was sealed. I'd need steam to open it without tearing the envelope. If it was evidence—which, considering that I got it from the Deputy Chief of the Santa Clara County Sheriff's Department, was a distinct possibility—and I opened it, I was fucking with the chain of custody. That would screw up whatever Cal was working on. It'd also cost me one of my best clients. Might land me in jail, or at least lose me my license.

I needed steam. Only one place around here I knew I could get that. I just needed to get back there with the envelope, and not get shot on the way.

Before all that is good and holy in this world, I fucking swear if I'd known I'd spend the day on a nature hike with a side order of gunfights, I'd have stayed in bed, and to hell with the lavish courier fees.

At least I didn't bring Klepto. He might look like he was rejected from Satan's puppy farm for being too monstrous, but his viscious streak extends just far enough to try to lick the gunmen to death.

But, you know? I'd have given anything to see that mutt right about now.

Two more minutes, I'd grabbed everything I was like to need from the wreck. Two from my stash of pre-paid phones—just in case one got shot or dunked in a stream—a messenger bag to carry the envelope in, and my lock picks, on the grounds that I didn't want to go crawling through any more windows.

Slide out of Francine. Leave her door soft-latched so I dodn't make any nose that would advertise my presence. Circle round to head up the hill so that I could get a clear cell signal...

...on second thought, maybe I oughta take a good look over Lynn and Jerry's Jeep before I head up. Might find something worth finding, something that might throw some light on this whole operation. Or at least give me a little more of a picture.

I had both earplugs out now, so I could hear anyone coming from a long ways off, at least if they weren't moving around in stealth mode.

Sounded mighty peaceful out there. The creek made a nice, pretty background noise. Some jays tweeted around the edges, gave the place the kind of atmosphere you found in those relaxation videos they used to sell on infomercials that ran at three in the morning back in the nineties. Not even any traffic on the road overhead. Rush hour was officially over.

Took a look under the Jeep again. Took a couple pics of the damage with the first pre-paid. Figured I oughta document the scene as it lay. Took a couple more photos of the rest of the scene—how they fell, the bullet holes, the slide marks coming down the hill. Best to have all this stuff documented for the insurance adjusters—and the DA, if it came to it. I wondered which end of that particular clusterfuck I might wind up on, then decided it didn't really matter if me and my two bodyguarding clients didn't make it through the rest of the day with our breathing apparatuses still functioning.

I tested the balance, decided I wouldn't tip the thing over even moving around, then climbed up into the Jeep.

Spooky in there. A living car has character, even when it isn't on. Dead cars...there's something about dead cars that's always creeped me out. They're like the perfect intersection between a human corpse and the uncanny valley. If I believed in ghosts—which I don't, because I just can't see God being that much of a dickhead—I'd have had that kind of feeling about dead cars that some people get about creepy not-quite-real sex dolls.

But that spooky feeling was stronger here. Made the hairs on my neck stand straight up. Found myself wondering if there were any other bombs in here that hadn't been tripped. Or if I'd noticed something wrong and didn't realize I'd noticed it.

I hate it when I do that. The rest of me always figures it out too late.

Found the reg and insurance card in the glove box, which I figured I'd need when the cops showed up. Lynn's cell was right underneath, in the passenger foot well, right where she said it oughta be. Nice big HTC. Not quite a tablet, but you could see there from here. She didn't have pockets that big. There had to be a purse in here somewhere, or an attaché case, or something. Maybe a laptop in a tote.

Found a couple laptops stowed in the pockets behind the seats. One for each of them. Thin ones. Looks like they had a Mac shop, which made me wonder about how serious they could actually be about their whole identity brokerage business.

That was something else I had to get into.

Meantime, I figured I might as well relieve the Jeep of its electronics. You never know what kind of disreputable characters might happen by. Motorists curious about skid marks. Mercenaries. Self-deluding whack-jobs who call themselves "private investigators." They went into my satchel.

Halfway out, I went back for the reg card and insurance. The way this morning was going, I'd forget to grab them when the tow truck came, and who knows how long it would be before Jerry got around to giving me his info. I stuck them in next to the electronics.

I went up the hill, giving the skid marks and footprints a wide berth. When the cops got here, they'd want to brush down the scene for anything that might help them ID the mercs and confirm my story about what went down, so I wasn't going to fuck up any more of it than I had to.

Three quarters of the way up. I had a satchel full of potential evidence, but no working address book. Time was, I carried a whole bloody Rolodex in my head. Now I have a cell phone. Or, *had* a cell phone. My whole contacts list was toast, and my backup was on the desktop at home. That leaves memory to work from.

I only knew three numbers by heart that'd do me any good.

"This is 911, what is your emergency?"

"I have an active shooter situation." I achieved the road. This time of day, you don't expect a whole lot out here, but right now it was all ghost highway. "Two gunmen, armed with short-barreled shotguns and handguns, hunting two civilians in and around the creek next to Pescadero Creek Road about a mile west of Macdonald County Park in San Mateo County."

"Sir, please identify yourself."

"Clarke Lantham, private investigator, license number FE 73645." The bad guys car was parked on the dirt shoulder on the far side of the road. I jogged across. "I'm somewhere on Pescadero Creek Road on the west side of the ridgeline in San Mateo county. There are two mercenaries loose in the area hunting two unarmed civilians. This is a contract kill situation. They were driving a black Ford Fusion, looks like a rental. Californa tags. License number 1LUN489."

"Are they in the car now?"

"No, the car is parked on a soft shoulder right next to where they ran another car off the road." I peered in the passenger window. Driver's side door looked like it was locked. So much for boosting their wheels. Not that it mattered, since I didn't have a spoof transponder key on me and wasn't up on boost techniques for the new Fords. "The gunmen are currently down slope in a gully. We've managed to dodge around them for now. Look, I need you to get people out here ASAP, okay?"

"Sir, please hold while I connect to dispatch."

Which is about what I figured.

I switched to speaker, locked the screen and slid that phone under my jacket, perched on my left shoulder. The weight of my left hand in my pocket kept it stationary, right where I could hear it without needing to trouble my busted wing about it.

Pulled out the other burner, dialed one of the only other two numbers I knew by heart that had any prayer in the world of getting me anywhere.

"Clarke Lantham Investigations."

"Nya, this is..."

"Clarke, oh my god. Are you okay? Where are you? I've been trying to find you everywhere. Lloyd's has been calling all morning and..."

"I'm in trouble. Lost my phone. This is one of the pre-paids. I don't have reliable reception right now, so I need you to take notes."

"Ready."

"Call Cal Oldman. Tell him I've been bushwhacked.

Something's going on with the job he's got me on. I've got two mercenaries hunting a pair of civilians out here. I've still got his package, haven't delivered it yet. I need help, bad. I'm outgunned. Give him this number. Tell him to run a locater on me. Text me if he needs consent, I'll do what I can to get. I need him out here now."

"Got it. Anything else?"

"Yeah. The civilians names: Lynnette Park and Gerald Manders. They run a startup called Personae. Think it might be important. After you talk to him, text me his cell number so I can contact him directly as soon as I get a chance, okay?"

"Okay. Clarke, be careful."

"Yeah, I'll do that. If Erica calls don't tell her anything's wrong, okay?"

"Clarke..."

"I mean it. Promise me. She'll land the whole Federal apparatus on my back, and I don't need them gumming up the works till I know those civilians are safe."

"I promise." She didn't sound very happy about it. "Come home alive?"

"I will."

"I love you, Clarke."

"Love you to. Gotta get moving." I hung up.

Felt kind of naked standing out there, in the one spot those guys were eventually guaranteed to come back to. Good way to wind up dead.

Still no sound from the 911 dispatcher in my other ear.

I needed to get out of sight. Somewhere I could keep a bead on this position and finish up with the phone business. Somewhere I could watch for the cavalry.

Somewhere I could keep myself from rattling apart.

I've been working on a theory for years now, that adrenaline poisoning is an actual condition that kills people. I figure about eight-five percent of all heart disease cases are due to people getting hooked on the stuff and forgetting to de-clench. If I'm right, I should die a nice peaceful chest-exploding death at about age fifty. Guess we'll find out, won't we?

I jogged down to the bridge, across it, about thirty yards from the Fusion. Scurried up the hill, found another bay tree.

The great thing about bay trees: not only do they smell like an Italian restaurant, they grow sideways, seeking out the light, so they're easy to climb and make great hunter's nests.

And I was hunting. Oh, brother, believe you me, I was gonna hunt these two-bit mercenary motherfuckers and get some answers if it was the last thing I did. Hearing Nya's voice, being reminded what it was that getting killed would make me leave behind, that pissed me off but royal.

On the other hand, they *did* smell like an Italian restaurant, and I was getting more than a little hungry.

"Hello," my shoulder said, "are you still there?"

"Yeah, I'm still here." I was talking quietly. Laying in wait, you push everything into stealth mode.

"We have units on route to you now. Please stay on the line until…"

"Sorry, can't. How long till they get here?"

"About twenty to thirty minutes."

"Peachy. Tell them when they get here that their suspects are two men, one about five ten, the other about six feet, both in their twenties, light brown complexions—mixed race—wearing Doc Martens, blue jeans, and Colombia windbreakers—black, one with blue trim and one with red trim. Be sure they get that description, I don't want them shooting me. I'm six three, whiter than an Irish ghost, wearing slate gray cargo pants, green t-shirt, black bomber jacket. Might as well send an ambulance, too. I've been shot—flesh wound, buckshot still in the wound, left tricep."

"Sir, I'm going to instruct you on first aid now..."

"I'm already bandaged with pressure and the bleeding's stopped, but I could really use some antibiotics and probably some stitches. You got all that?"

"Yes."

"Good. I'm hanging up now. Don't call me back. The sound of the ringer might tell them where I am, and I really don't want to get killed. I've got an eye on the Fusion, I'll come out when the cops get here."

I hung up before she could say anything else. She was going to try to keep me on the line. That was her job. The cops weren't going to like the notion that I was hiding with eyes on their landing spot, but they could just fucking deal with it. They've got armored vests for a reason, let 'em earn their hazard pay.

Me? I needed to find out who these sheep fuckers were and get the drop on them. There's only one man I knew who could help me—thank God his number is number three on the list of those I've had to actually dial enough that I have it burned into my brain meats.

Ring ring.

Click.

"Thrill me, baby." Earl Whitaker. Top notch data miner—a lot of my expense money goes to him. The kind of guy who makes a few hundred million in a startup and uses it to build a palace where he can dress in the latest designer lingerie and hack into any computer system on the planet. The kind of guy that makes friendly governments wet their bed, when they're not pitching contracts his way.

"Earl, this is Lantham."

"Clarkie boy blue, let me blow your horn."

"Flattered. What do you know about Persona?"

"It's something you need, sweetie. Style, flash, a little squiggle in those hips..."

"I think you've got enough for any five of me."

"Believe it, Bo Peep."

"It's some kind of blockchain thing. Identity brokerage. I need to know everything you can about what they're doing, and who's trying to buy them."

"Oh, honey, when are you gonna bring me a hard one?"

"Will see what I can do. What'll this cost me?"

"For you, Clarkie boy, not a lot."

"So, only four zeroes?"

"Maybe two or three. I'll knock it out this afternoon between my squash game and my..."

"Yeah, yeah, I know. Thanks, Earl. You're tops."

"For you, my boy, always. Keep your head unfucked."

"I'll do what I can. Send everything to Nya, will you?"

"Easier done than said. Ta-ta."

So now all I had to do was wait. I hate waiting. Nya, where the hell are you?

She should have sent that message by...

Ding ding.

...now. And I haven't turned the ringer off. Probably woke up every Stellar's jay for a mile. If that muscle was anywhere nearby, I was blown.

Fuck.

Checked the message.

Left a message for Cal. He's not answering.

In the middle of my next volley of mental profanity, the phone beeped again, cause I still hadn't turned off the goddamn ringer.

Cal's contact info. Great. Save the vcard. Yes, I want to add it to my fucking contact list already.

God what I wouldn't give to resurrect my phone.

Now, menu. Settings.

Where did they hide the *Turn off the fucking homing device for bad guys with guns button?*

Stupid specialized interfaces. Why bother on a phone that costs fifty bucks, for fuck's sake?

Movement.

Up the road.

Check the movement.

There they are. Both of them. The mercs.

LITTLE RED HANGING BACK on the hill, providing cover.

Papa Smurf did a quick jog across the road to the Fusion, popped the trunk. Grabbed something out of it, couldn't tell what. Whatever it was, it wasn't big. Not a bag. Small enough that he could carry it in his left back across the road.

His pockets were full, too. Dude was packing some extra gear.

He got back to Little Red, and the two of them skedaddled down the hill again. They were still on the hunt, which meant Lynn and Jerry had got away clean. Some comfort there.

On the other hand, they were back in the game, and they were right here. If I could keep 'em local, I'd have a lot easier time getting them arrested.

I slipped off the trunk. Bumped my arm on the way down. Hurt like hell. It was starting to swell. Whatever shock I'd been in had passed off, so I wasn't worried about permanent damage, but holy bloody fucking Christ, it felt like someone lit a bruise on fire and left it to smolder.

My wounds and cargo and I all shuffled across the road. I wasn't moving slow, but I sure wasn't moving fast. Before I got to the far side, my nose caught the sharp, spiny smell of burning plastics.

No no no oh come on! Somewhere in my soul, the little four year old I keep around to tell me about when life is unfair was screaming his little head off, running around in circles, and stomping a lot.

He got louder when the smoke got thick enough for me to actually see it—streaks of black billowing through the mist.

They'd killed Francine. I knew it. They torched the Jeep and the Subaru. Everything I still had in her was gone. All the little equipment stashes. The custom work I'd sunk into her.

I got my head over the edge. I could see all the way down now. Wished I couldn't. Yeah, Francine was dead. The kind of dead even Jacob Marley couldn't come back from. They'd torched her. Torched 'em both. Torched 'em good. Thick black petroleum-fed smoke shat its way into the sky from the hollowed-out iron skeletons already scorched completely black. Five'll get you ten, a couple of road flares and a bottle of rye or a rag. Doesn't take much to send a box of hydrocarbons wafting skyward like a sacrifice to the god of all gearboxes.

Fucking car-murdering bastards.

Well, Francine died in the line of duty. Maybe I could claim her on my business insurance if Jerry's insurance didn't make with the claim check. *Note to self: check to see if malicious arson is covered on the hazard policy.*

I spent a good three seconds standing at the top of that grade seething. Reminding myself that revenge for car murder is not a legal justification for homicide. You think I'm joking, but at that point, for those few seconds, I really did have to remind myself that just because I was carrying two guns did not mean I actually get to kill people, no matter how richly they deserved it. If nothing else, I'd lose my insurance.

I'd probably go to jail, too, since I wasn't a cop anymore so the police union wouldn't cover my ass if I want on a recreational murder spree.

Movement down near the trucks. Papa Smurf and Little Red, plain as day. The fog was just atmosphere now.

"Hey!" I shouted. "Are you guys okay?"

One of them shifted his weight. Spotted it before I knew what it meant. Cold sweat on the back of my neck.

I ate pavement. Gun out of the back holster. Satchel smashing the ground next to me. Here's hoping those laptops could stand a little abuse.

Here's hoping I saved them from getting hit.

Pop pop pop

Slugs zipped past me. Three of them. Like little wasps pushed out of a slingshot. Tearing little chunks out of the edge of the hillside six inches from my right side.

Then they stopped.

Trigger discipline. Always a bad thing in an opponent.

Come on, Lantham, get lost. Laying down here I was either at stalemate or I was dead. If they took off, I wouldn't be able to follow them, not from here.

I rolled out into traffic, or at least into where the traffic is supposed to go when you're not out in the middle of nowhere. Came up in a crouch, stayed low.

The crash site was across the road from a steep cliff cut into the hillside. The Fusion was parked over there. The car they came in. The curve wasn't sharp enough to merit a guard rail, which is how we sailed down it so easy. But that meant there wasn't a lot of cover with good vantage. About my only option as about ten yards uphill, where the stream crossed under the road and the road switched sides on the canyon. Up there, my side of the road ran smack into a hill, and that hill had scrub oaks on it, which make for pretty decent cover.

Low, quick run. Got up behind a tree in five seconds flat.

Good thing I did. They were climbing the hill to find me. I was now officially a loose end.

That's right, that's right. Come on, guys. I've got more range and less drop in this .45 than you've got in that little shorty nine.

Granted, that sawed-off Mossberg could pretty much blast me across the road from twenty-five yards, but that's why I was going to take that guy out first. I squeezed the plugs into my ears. Just in case.

They hadn't spotted me. They got to the top of the hill and did a good two-man sweep around. Their eyes went right past me two or three times, but with only my eyeballs poking out from behind the crook of a limb, they didn't make me, thank God.

After about thirty seconds, they decided I'd managed an escape somehow.

And they made a beeline for the car.

Both of them had their backs to me. And they were well within range.

I dropped the satchel. Slipped out from behind the tree. Closed the gap with low soft quick steps.

.45 high. Arm's length. Right at their backs.

When I got inside eight yards, I scuffed my right shoe against the ground. It got their attention.

They both checked back.

"I'm guessing you guys know that deer aren't made of metal and setting them on fire isn't the best way to get venison. No, don't turn around. Just stay still. Nice. Just like that." I said it in the kind of tone that makes people afraid to reach for their guns. "You know, if I can get through the day without killing anyone, I'd call it a win. Maybe you can help me with that."

"Who the hell *are* you?" Little Red. On the left. He was packing the shorty.

"Me? I'm just a traffic accident waiting to happen. Thanks for the buckshot, by the way. I was feeling a little numb in that arm. Now drop the hardware."

Going just on the distinct lack of weapons clattering on the tarmac, they didn't seem like they were in a hell of a hurry to avoid getting shot.

"You know, I get awful nervous when people don't do what they're told. Makes me kinda twitchy. When I'm twitchy, weird shit tends to..." I squeezed the trigger and sent a warning shot into the cliff behind the car, "...happen. Like that. I mean, guns have minds of their own. That can't be a good thing, right? Now, drop the shit and let's have a little chat."

They both dropped their weapons. The Little Red squatted down and laid a Glock at his feet. Papa Smurf used two fingers around the barrel to lay his pistol-grip Mossberg down like the asphalt was a feather pillow.

"Step away. This way. Two steps. One more. Good. Now, what brings a couple punks out here to play with guns?" I knew it would get under their skin. Whether they're stone cold psychos or macho assholes, the one place you can needle guys like this is in the ego.

Both of them were too smart, or too well-trained, to say anything. Name, rank, and serial number is all I'd get out of them if they were active duty military on a legal assignment. Situation like this, I figured I'd be lucky to get a fart. But I had to keep them interested. And I had to get them away from their guns. Then I needed to stall them. *911 dispatch, don't fail me now.*

"I hate to do this. I really do. I hate to interfere with my fellow freelancers. But I am gonna have to arrest you both." After all this time, you think I'd pack handcuffs. Sometimes, I'm a little slow on the uptake. Which Rachael reminds me of. All the time. At volume nine. Maybe there were some upsides to her doing the runner.

Then again, if she was here, she'd probably have a pair on her. She likes to travel with emergency toys. Always prepared in the event of impromptu debauchery. She's a regular boy scout like that.

"You are?" Little Red had that ash tray voice. Straight from film trailers. Made me wish I was in a world filled with danger where nothing is what it seems, until one man changes everything through sheer courage and determination.

I wasn't though, all I had was a .45 and a bucketload of irritation. "Back up, have a seat on the trunk." *Let's just wait for the cavalry, boys.*

"I don't think so." Papa Smurf was looking at me in a way that made me feel distinctly unsafe.

Mister Lantham, for the record, did you feel yourself in immanent danger of life and limb when you shot the victim?

Why yes, Mr. District Attorney, I did. Dude was looking at me funny.

Yeah, I didn't think it'd wash either. I had to persuade them.

"Suit yourself. You walk out or you can get airlifted after the cougars have at you. Your choice." Lantham the diplomat, that's me. If I'd been the ambassador to Russia in the fifties, humanity would never have had to suffer through the *Star Wars* prequels.

But these guys didn't believe me. Not a credible threat? I was taller than either of them, mean enough to be on their team, and I was the one holding a gun. Try as I might, I just couldn't see a good reason why they didn't want to take me seriously.

Until I heard rubber scuff against the tarmac behind me.

I dropped. They dropped.

Someone behind me let a shot off. I didn't wait to see who. Papa Smurf got his hands on the 12 guage. I squeezed. He crumpled, fell sideways. I popped off four more rounds in a sweep at Little Red and whoever was behind me.

Only needed two seconds. You can buy two seconds with a few rounds. If you're lucky.

I wasn't about to bank on luck. I dove straight at Papa Smurf. Grabbed his body. I'd gotten him through the neck.

He wasn't quite dead yet.

I yanked him up and huddled behind him, dragged him to the car. He tried getting around on me, clawing at me, grabbing me, trying to take me with him as he bled out through the big gash in his neck. Washing my open wounds in the blood of the Smurf.

You better not have AIDS, buddy, or I'll kill you all over again.

The air crackled. So many shots I couldn't count 'em. I could feel the thump through his body as the friendly fire slugs slammed into him. If they'd been firing magnum loads I'd have gotten sloppy seconds when the bullets went through-and-through.

It got me to the car, though. And behind it. I left the corpse at the rear wheels, got behind the engine. Ducked down and looked under the car.

The gunfire had stopped. I heard mags changing. I couldn't see feet, so they had to be right behind the wheels on the other side. Any minute, the two of them, if they had any brains, would be coming at me from different ends. One from the front, one from the back, Papa Smurf's still-convulsing body playing speed bump.

I had maybe eight seconds of life left in me. Not a good day to be a Lantham, no sirree.

Be sure to get checked for HIV and Hep-C if you get out of here, Lantham. That's my sister talking. She's a nurse. I keep some recordings of her voice in the back of my head, special, for situations like this. It's optimistic. If I actually lasted long enough to get either of those diseases, I'd be luckier than a guy who wins the lottery every time he plays the numbers his cellmate tattooed on his scrotum.

I took two seconds to change mags myself. I wasn't out, but I was down to three rounds, and it looked like I was about to need every squeeze I could get. I put the half-mag back in the belt, then checked back under the car.

Still no feet.

They had to be behind the wheels. They weren't very big wheels. Sixteen inchers. And rubber sidewalls don't stop bullets.

I had a better angle on the back tire. I aimed right through it, and squeezed off two.

A Glock clattered to the ground. A man howled, a voice so high I figured it had to be the new guy. Little Red couldn't get his voice that high if I castrated him.

If I'd gotten him in the ankle, he was out of play. If I'd hit the muscle, he could still be in. I sure as hell wasn't going to stand up to check.

Swung the 1911 to the other tire, but not before slugs started plugging the car above me. Bastard was firing at an angle, trying to get me through the body work over the engine. Only reason they didn't go through *my* body work was that I was on my stomach huddled in as close as I could.

Curled my legs in anyway. Reflex. Just in case they weren't clear.

I fired twice at the front tire. They both plinked off the inside of the wheel.

The adrenaline was getting to me. Fucking up my aim. Dammit.

"Hey! Who's over there? Clarke? Clarke is that you?" Jerry's voice, coming from somewhere. Earplugs made it seem really far off. It wasn't possible to tell where hew as in this canyon. Voice seemed to come from everywhere at once. But above the road, for sure.

Goddammit, Jerry, don't you know a firefight when you hear one?

"Hold it." The voice from the back wheel. Gritted teeth. A medium tenor. Absolutely nondescript voice.

"Clarke! Clarke are you down there?"

"Hill?" Came Little Red's voice.

"Go." The other man picked up the Glock.

"Burke?"

"He's not going anywhere."

The car shifted. The new guy had crawled up on the trunk. He was getting in position to take me out, or at least pin me down.

On the other hand, it meant I only had one of them to worry about.

The car shifted a last time. It bore his full weight now. He was on the trunk.

I moved. Rolled around the front. Not easy to keep my head low when you're as tall as I am, but I managed somehow. Little Red was out of sight already, must've ducked over the edge of the hill, banking that Jerry was somewhere up the cliff on the far side of the creek. I only had to worry about the asshole behind me. Ain't that sweet.

Goddammit, where the hell are the cops?

This is the part of our program where our intrepid detective turns to the camera and asks "What would you do?" He doesn't do it because he's trying to include you, give you a drinking game to play along at home, that kind of thing. He's doing it because he hasn't got a goddamn clue and he figures that asking leading questions of someone else will make him look smarter than he is and give him a leg up, let him come out ahead. Usually I've got a sidekick for that, goddammit.

I could hunker down. Try to wait him out. Trade shots, maybe get lucky and put my man down. But I didn't know how much ammo he had in reserve.

Except...maybe I did.

He was carrying a Glock. I'd seen it. He was firing 9mm shorts, I'd heard them. Double-stack subcompact that caliber, that meant a model 25, maybe 28. Looked like a 25, though. Drug runner's gun. Popular in Mexico. Illegal for import into the US except for military and police. Hard to get your hands on in San Diego, easy as burping in Tijuana.

Great, Lantham, one more fact that confirms what you already knew.

How many rounds had he fired? Four, maybe. Maybe less. That mag carried fifteen. Add one in the pipe, you get twice what I can fit in my 1911 at full top-off.

So he had more goes than I did. And more training than I did. And I had no way of knowing how many extra mags he had in his pocket. I only had thirty-two rounds left across both guns. He could carry that much in one pocket. I know a losing proposition when I smell it.

The car shifted again. He was moving. Over the top, or around the side? Either way, if I played circle-the-car with this bozo, I was going to end up too dead to wait for the cops.

If I couldn't out-shoot him, maybe I could pin him.

"Hey! You on the other side of the car!"

"Yeah?"

"You come out right now, I'll let you live." I wasn't carrying my dental mirror. Didn't have most of my normal bag of tricks. I splayed down, try to see if he'd come down anywhere. I could see a little movement behind the twitching corpse.

"Sounds like a fair offer."

"I'll even throw in lunch," I pulled up to a squat, "If you tell me who hired you. Hell, I won't even arrest you."

"What, you some kind of cop?"

"Something like that." I pushed myself up and popped two off in his direction. He dropped. Couldn't tell if I hit him. I started backpedalling, hard, skipping right, fading as fast as I could. He popped up again, I laid another one at him. I was down to one.

He dropped again. I was close enough to the edge of the hill to make a hard dash for it. Figured I'd better, before he used on me the same trick I used to lame him. Had to bank on him not being able to run fast enough to catch me.

Couldn't bank on him missing me at this range, even

with that pop gun. I holstered the 1911 and took out the .357. Enough hard firepower to punch through the whole back end of that car without tumbling.

I aimed for the back of the car, made a best guess for where he was crouching.

Fired.

Heard a yelp. That was all I needed.

I turned, sprinted the last fifteen feet to the soft shoulder on the other side, and dove over the cliff.

11:10 AM. THURSDAY

I ROLLED DOWN, CAME OUT in an ass-skid. The ground was drier now than it had been this morning. Hard to slide far on dry ground. I rolled back to my feet and kept on running down the hill. Right toward the bonfire.

Once I hit the bottom, I put the fire between myself and the uphill. Did my best not to breathe that shit. Enough heat pouring off it to melt diamonds. The stream sizzled, fingers of steam licked up from underneath to join the smoke.

Eight minutes.

According to the call log on the pre-paid, that's all the time that had passed since I called 911.

I wasn't even halfway to cavalry-land yet. And I still had two wild civilians on the loose, who I needed to catch before they happened upon some innocent passer-by. Never underestimate the predatory instincts of panicked people lost in the woods. I didn't just learn that from watching too many slasher movies as a kid, either. Frightened people—especially people who are being hunted and aren't trained to deal with fear—can do incredibly destructive things, because they're not thinking straight.

Getting rid of the gunman would be nice too. I figured I only had one left to deal with, what with the one being dead and the second one having one hole in his foot and another he'd picked up when I shot through the trunk. He wasn't going to be doing a lot of moving anytime soon. So long as I stayed out of line-of-sight of that car, I oughta be okay.

Now, to figure where Jerry had gone. And Little Red. Following footprints wasn't going to do me any good, even if I wasn't shit at tracking. Between me and the bad guys and the Jeep refugees, the ground around these cars looked like someone had been playing BART station.

Little Red wasn't more than a minute ahead of me, and the gunfire might draw him back. He might be thinking his buddy finished me off—or that his buddy needed help. He could appear from out the trees any second, send me off to old man death, and I couldn't do a thing about it.

Time to get away from the wreck and into a covered position.

So I got a good run going and plowed into the forest on the hillside. Steep climb. Not straight up, but you could see there from here. The trees made for a kind of hand-over-hand climb up maybe a fifty or sixty degree grade, between the bay and the redwoods and over the occasional poison oak brambles.

Whatever you do, Lantham, don't touch your pant legs or shoes. Especially not in the bathroom.

I'm not all that allergic, but there's no sense in tempting fate, right?

Five more minutes of hard climb. Thirteen minutes of the twenty-to-thirty. The cops might as well be two hours away. I found a wide trail running across the face of the mountain—wide enough that, for all I know, it might be the driveway for that house we hid out in earlier.

I scrambled up over the bank, took some cover, turned around, got a look behind me.

Couldn't see a hell of a lot through the smoke. I'd picked a good spot to climb, I was out of the visual field from the guy I'd left by the car. Now I needed to make sure he was still there.

Shuffled along the road. Heading west from one tree to another, staying under cover from the one direction I was sure mattered. Got clear of the smoke.

Looking back at the car, I'll give this to the guy with the bullets in him: he had a lot of grit. I don't know how he did it, but he wasn't anywhere I could see him, which meant that he had to either be pursuing me on foot, or he'd fled into the trees, too.

Wondered if the bad guys had radio linkups. Help them coordinate their movements. Might explain where the third guy came from.

Doesn't explain where he went, though.

Or where I could find Jerry. Or Lynn. Or Little Red.

Ring. Ring.

Ring.

It wasn't actually a ring like an old fashioned telephone. It was one of those unbearable generic ring tones like you get on pre-paid cell phones. The kind that announces to gunmen everywhere exactly where you're hiding out, particularly when you're the kind of idiot who forgets to turn off the fucking ringer. A special kind of idiot. Lantham the Idiot, in caps.

Idiot is an honorary title bestowed upon me by an old girlfriend who got annoyed with the number of times I come close to meriting a morticians attention in any given calendar month.

I fumbled it out of my pocket. I didn't recognize the number, but since I didn't actually have a directory on this phone that didn't mean a hell of a lot.

"Lantham. Make it fucking quick."

"Lantham, it's Cal."

"Cal, you got Nya's message?"

"I did."

"Get the fuck up here. I've got a team of three mercenaries hunting me and two civilians, and we've been separated. One of the mercs is down, another one's been shot but is still on the move."

Cal swore in a way that made me understand a lot more about Rachael's vocabulary.

"Yeah, that's about the shape of it. I gotta go. I'm in and out of cell range, but you can't miss the location. There's a big black plume of smoke where two cars are trying to set the forest on fire in the creek, and another car up on the road with a dead body by its rear tires. Just get me air support and some cops out here, okay?"

"I got you. Clarke..."

"Yeah."

"The package."

"Never made it. I saved it from the wreck. Oh, that reminds me."

"Yeah?"

"These civilians. Manders and Park? They were meeting with Ferris this morning..."

He did that cute swearing thing again. Never seen the guy go round the bend before. Gotta admit, it had its appeal knowing it was possible to rattle him. At this point, it didn't scare me, on the grounds that I wasn't sure I was going to live long enough to get scared by whatever had his panties in a bunch. If I did live long enough, though, I was pretty sure I wasn't going to like the answers I found.

"Understand something, Clarke. I don't care what you have to do, I don't care who you have to kill. You keep them alive." he said.

"That's a hell of a blank check. Who are these people?"

"The kind of people who upset apple carts."

"Must be a hell of an apple cart."

"They're worth the trouble."

"Coulda fooled me. What do they know? What do they have on you?"

"It's not what they have on me I'm worried about. Now get moving. Whatever you have to do, I'll cover your ass."

"You will, huh. That might be a lot of trouble you're buying. So far I've got one body on deck, and it was a clean shoot, but..."

"Lantham. You're covered."

"You leave me holding the bag on this one, Cal, and you ain't gonna like me much."

"I got you."

"Yeah, okay. Get the fuck out here, will ya?"

"I'll text you when I'm on site."

Click.

Not that he'll be in charge, since I'm in San Mateo County. Let's hope his years of seniority have earned him good will with the local fuzz.

I took two minutes to balance my ammo. I topped off the revolver, cannibalized a round from one of my speedloaders to do it. Then shuffled ammo around in my .45 mags so that I had a full clean reload on top of the four rounds already in the gun. The empties went into the belt pouches that were harder to reach. No reason to give myself more of a pain in the arm than I'd need to.

Eleven shots total for the 1911, seventeen for the snubbie. Not a hell of a lot. It's never a good day when your chances of survival are based on how well you can count explosions.

Strategy time. I needed to find these fuckers. If the dead body had coms on it, I could use that. But I'd have to climb down, then up again, waste another few minutes doing it.

So how else was I going to find them?

Well, sometimes, you gotta just throw it to the wind and do something unbearably stupid.

"Jerry!" I bellowed at the top of my lungs. Even irritable as they were due to all the chemical smoke, I still yelled loud enough to scare birds out of the trees on the other side of the canyon. "Lynn! Can you hear me?"

Nothing for a second or two.

Then: "Help! Help! Aaaaaaaaaah"

I'VE HEARD A LOT OF "AAAHS" in my time. That one wasn't the kind of "aaaah" that people scream in movies when they go off a cliff. More the kind that someone screams when they're trying to yell to attract attention but they don't have any good words.

Up here, the acoustics were a lot better. About forty feet above the road, on a continuous hill face, I had a better chance of guessing which way it was coming from.

Downstream, definitely. I drew my 1911 and held it low-ready,

Time to go for a jog.

I didn't yell out that I was coming, and they should hang in there. I didn't tell them to be brave, or hide out, or do anything to reassure them. There were three reasons for this: first, I didn't care whether they were scared or not, and second, I'm not in a movie where I have to make the audience feel some kind of emotional connection with the hero, and third, which I know is going to shock you:

I am not an idiot.

I'm not the only guy with a gun out here, and I'd rather the other guys with guns didn't have a chance to figure out what direction I was coming from.

The road snaked around the mountain, heading almost level out to the west. If it kept going too long without making a solid turn it'd be forced to resort to bridges or a ramp to launch me into the Pacific Ocean, but there were about ten-as-the-crow-flies miles before I really had to worry about ruining my sneakers in salt water instead of fresh water.

Weird as it sounds, the jog helped. Burned off enough adrenaline that it put a damper on the shakes. The shakes are the worst part of life-and-death. It fucks up your aim and does the same kinds of things to your judgment that alcohol does, except it makes you jittery instead of mellow. I was hurting and tired, hungry enough to eat a water buffalo and thirsty enough to drink the water that it's named after, but a quarter-mile along, I was feeling pretty limber.

I kept my eyes on the creek bed. That asshole that I plugged had to be down there somewhere, limping along, doing his heroic best to finish his mission and get home in only three pieces. He couldn't have gotten that far ahead of me.

But I didn't see him. I started to wonder if some cosmic Bugs Bunny was dotting the world with wormholes, and everyone else knew the fast way through the maze but me.

Coming round the point of the next bend, though, I saw, across a gap between curves, bits of a house peeking out between the trees. Looked like the same house where we'd hidden out before. Following my memory downslope, I found the finger of granite we'd crawled up.

That was the place. The shout had come from up here somewhere, so where...

There. I spotted them. Directly across the from me, clinging to the downhill side of the mountain, a little ways below the road. Hiding in the lee of a fallen redwood. Both of them down there.

Why the hell hadn't they gotten out when they could?

I tracked up. Little Red was creeping along the road toward the house, above them. He wasn't very far ahead of me, now. Maybe a couple hundred yards, the way the road travels. I just had to come up behind him, get his gun, knock him over.

Before I did that, I needed to turn off my ringers. I paged through the first pre-paid, found the ringer button, muted it and turned off the buzz. Did the same thing with the second one. Now I didn't have to worry about Cal texting and announcing my position to someone who was itching to put me in the ground.

Now that the cat wasn't belled, he could pussyfoot his way up to the mouse.

Ugly damn mouse. No mouse has that kind of fashion sense. Who in the hell wears a red-trimmed black hiking jacket to perform a hit in the woods? Black might be urban camo—at night, if you're laying face down on an unlit street—but it shows up against the forest background almost as well as neon orange, a fact I'd been way too aware of all morning, moving around in my leather jacket.

His mistake. Easier for me.

He was making a careful go of it. Time to bite him on the ass.

Figuratively speaking. I wasn't *that* hungry yet.

Now, for the record, here's what I should have done once I closed to within ten yards:

Shoot him in the back, three times.

But I am conditioned from an early age not to kill people when they're not looking. It's unsporting. And I don't want to find out what it feels like. Killing someone fair and square is already unpleasant enough. It's also murder, and most DAs I know tend to frown on that kind of thing.

So I didn't do that. But I should have.

I told him to stop. To toss the piece. To sink to his knees. Put his hands behind his head. I didn't know how I was gonna tie him up yet, but I figured it was a good start. Maybe I could use a shoelace.

He did what I told him to do. He already knew I had no compunction about shooting him. I'd shot two of his buddies in the last ten minutes, and he'd been there for both of them.

I circled around to his right so I could pick up his gun, stayed well back. This put my back to the open sky. Another decision I'd take a do-over on if I had the chance.

"What's your name?"

"Fuck off."

"Okay, Fuck—do you mind if I call you Fuck? Mr. Off seems too formal for hanging around in the woods."

"Fuck off. God."

"Yeah, yeah, you told me your name already. But I'm Clarke. So next time I ask 'What's your name?' you can say 'Fuck Off, Clarke', and we'll be good. But since I've got your name already, try telling me who hired you."

He didn't say anything.

"Come on, I know you know English. I bet you even know how to read. I mean, it's not like you're a Marine, you've actually got brains."

He growled without intending to. Well, that told me where he got his training. If he'd laughed, that would've meant Army or SEALs.

"Oh, you are? Well, look, I'm sorry, really. Hey, tell you what. My mom told me I used to shit my pants at preschool, and that's almost as bad, so if you don't tell anyone, neither will I."

He was getting pissed. It occurred to me that pissing off a Marine might not be the best way to keep people alive. I considered mentioning that the cops were coming, but that would increase any escape urgency he was feeling. Might as well back off a bit, leave him some breathing room. Untie my shoes.

I did just that. Backed off, sat down with my back to the air.

Christ, Lantham, even Bozo the Clown's retarded hamster isn't that stupid! I hear you say. Or, rather, I would hear Rachael say, if she was here, which she isn't. If she was...goddammit. I don't even want to think about it. But she'd say something like: *Make him give you his shoelaces, don't use yours. And don't ever sit with your back unprotected against the open air!!!*

Well, in my defense, I hadn't had anything to eat or drink, I needed to piss, I had lost Francine on a completely unnecessary funeral pyre, I'd been shot, shot at, ambushed, chased, stood up by cops, woken up at four in the morning by my ex-assistant's deputy dog dad, and now I was stuck in the middle of nowhere with one prisoner, no backup, and no cuffs, so I'll thank you to cut down on the smart ass remarks. I get enough of those from myself.

I collected the loose gun. Glock 25. Stuffed it in my pocket. Then I pulled the loop-string on my left shoelace.

This is the point in our story where I need to explain something to those of you in the audience who were never infected with the ballistics bug. For me, it started when I was six and figured out that I could knock pinecones of redwood trees with my sister's BB gun. It's been more-or-less downhill from there, which is probably a good thing when I consider my chosen profession.

The thing you don't really get a feel for when you're watching movies is how far bullets fly, and what they can do. Most bullets from most guns will travel a mile or two if they don't happen to run into anyone while they're out for their little stroll—but that doesn't mean the asshole that actually pulled the trigger is going to hit anything except the occasional road sign. If you want the slug to actually land on the thing you're pointing your gun at, and that thing is more than about thirty feet away, you have to do three things: You have to aim. You have to not jerk your hand when you squeeze. And you have to have a bullet that's not going to tumble and drop for a long ways.

If your bullet isn't going faster than the speed of sound, then you're probably out of luck. Subsonic rounds—like my .45, or the 9mm shorts like the bad guys here are using—tend to skew off course pretty quick, and you have to be really, *really* good to compensate for that. It also helps if you've got a longer barrel—they make the bullet fly a little faster and a little straighter, so you got a better chance of hitting what you're aiming at.

On a good day at the range, with my target sights, I can reliably hit the center at fifty yards with my 1911. I can't do that in combat, not with adrenaline and combat sights on the weapon. But fifty yard headshots with a .45 is what what other cops call "fucking crazy," because the .45 is strictly a short range round.

Same with the heat these guys were packing.

That's why I heard the gunshot before the bullet whizzed past my head. And that's why I barely managed not to get dead with Mr. Limpy unloading at the hillside from the spot where I'd just sized up Little Red from not three minutes ago.

Suddenly I've got all my attention absorbed in trying not to get dead. Little Red gets up, lunges for me, I notice just in time to point the barrel at him, and then his buddy sends a few hunks of lead between us, which made me dive for cover again. Made Little Red turn tail and run. Either Limpy got exactly what he was hoping for, or Little Red was gonna introduce him to the wonderful world of extra orifices when he got back to the car. Either way, it was a ballsy move. At that range, I wouldn't've trusted myself not to hit the guy on my team.

Limpy, across the way, was in the Fusion. Drove it up the road to avoid the whole limping thing, was firing at me from out of the passenger window. This dirt road must be that house's driveway, must connect to the main drag a little ways up the hill from where the car crash happened.

Not just firing at me, though. Firing at the two on the hillside below me.

"Jerry! Lynn! You two okay down there?"

"Lantham?" Lynn's voice.

"Last time I checked." I popped a round off at the bad guys, didn't even hit the car. Shaking too much. The shot went wild and up to the left. Saw the redwood bark splinter.

I really need more range time. Guess I shouldn't've stopped going when Rachael lit out on me.

"Where are they?" Lynn said

"Right across from you, up on the road. I'd get under come cover if I was you."

There was a lot of "oh shit"ing and "ow"ing and "oof"ing and "ak"ing too, in between all the lovely gunfire from the other side. Only bright spot in the whole mess was that they were burning through ammo and not hitting a bloody thing.

Suppressing fire? Were they trying to scare us all up onto the road?

Maybe. But up here, they were just as vulnerable as we were. Maybe more vulnerable. I had a pretty good notion that I knew the terrain a lot better than them by this point. Might be able to use it to my advantage.

First, I had to spend the rest of the magazine getting them to duck, so my charges could get up the hill without getting their wings. If my .357 snubbie had a good five or six inch barrel, I'd use it. Might actually be able to pick them both off instead of trusting to luck. As it was, I was getting close—paying attention to the drop, adjusting my aim, leading in, getting closer with every squeeze—but I wasn't kidding myself. I was rattled enough that if I actually landed a hit on either of them it'd be blind luck.

Almost literally, since I was shooting without so much as a pair of sunglasses on for eye protection.

And I was starting to run low on ammo. On my last mag. Five shots left now. After that, it was seventeen for the revolver, plus whatever was left in that Glock, then I was spent. These fuckers were gonna burn through my whole stash if I wasn't careful.

Time for a different plan. What I really needed was someone else who knew how to handle themselves in a firefight. With two, I could keep their attention while my partner flanked them.

Except my partner was off somewhere trying to "find herself." *Rachael, you picked a hell of a time to go and prove the stereotype about the dippiest features of the Californian psyche.*

Lynn yelped somewhere below me and to my left.

Guess that's my exit cue.

"What's up?"

"I'm hit!" Lynn said, obviously not happy about it, but at least she as talking, so there might be time to keep her on this side of the Valhalla.

"Get under cover!"

"What does that mean?" Jerry shouted.

"It means get something solid between you and the bad guys." Speaking of bad guys, one of them was popping up to take another plug at my clients. I took careful aim, managed to carom a shot off the car only an inch or so from his shoulder. Next shot I might actually hit with. "Something that'll stop bullets. A big tree, a log, a rock, anything like that." *Lantham, remember this moment if you're ever tempted to teach kindegarten-level physics professionally.*

Another way you could tell these guys were pros: They weren't rushing me with their car. They knew as well as I did that if they drove at me, I'd just kill the pair of 'em easy as giving my bratwurst two shakes after pissing in a baseball park. So they didn't. They kept up with the plinking, kept me pinned down. There wasn't as much of it now as there was a moment ago, which meant that Little Red had probably re-armed and was sneaking around again. My position wasn't going to be safe for much longer—if he climbed high and came at me from the cover of the forest above, I was gonna have a new waste disposal window in my stomach pretty damn quick.

I holstered the .45. It wasn't quite dead, but I didn't want to be carrying around a useless hunk of hardware, and I sure as hell didn't want to throw it away. I've been through too much with that piece. Makes me kind of sentimental. Not like I get over cars, but still, a little sentimental all the same.

I drew the .357, and wished once again I'd at *least* gotten a Model 60 instead of this ridiculous little cannon with the two inch barrel. I'd be lucky if I could hit the broad side of the Goodyear blimp with this thing.

But it had more ammo, and it did have faster slugs. I figured it might make an impact.

I backed along the road till I was about directly above Jerry and Lynn.

"You guys okay down there?"

"Yeah," Lynn grunted. She couldn't be that far down, even.

"Okay. Hold on."

I backed up a little more, scooted to behind the neared convenient tree, looked down.

They were about ten feet below me. A tangle of roots fell off the remains of a landslide where a scrub oak clung to the edge of the dirt road. She must've gotten shot trying to climb up. There was no cover down there, and I could see the Fusion straight shot over. Anyone sitting in or behind that car had a clear shot.

Well, they weren't going to for long. There are a couple things you can do to compensate having to shoot a handgun at range. I crouched in the lee of that scrub oak, laid down on my belly, rested the butt of the .357 on the ground, propped the frame against the trunk. Got it dead-rock stable. Lined that cab right up behind my sights.

One round downrange. Two. Three. The driver's side door opened up. Bodies moved on the far side. Four. Five. They were out of sight.

Alright Lantham, drop over that cliff now. I palmed the revolver in my left hand, dove forward, caught the roots with my right, swung down. Dropped the eight feet into the soft forest bedding that coated the hillside. Dropped, rolled, had to worry about stopping, then had to worry about my chiropractor bill when a redwood sapling caught me in the back.

"Ugh. I have got to find another line of work."

Well, I say that, but at this point, between getting drummed out of the Oakland PD—and you know when a town has its policing license revoked twice in ten years by the Feds for civil rights violations, getting fired from it is not quite the kind of accomplishment you want to list on a resume—and running my own business for the last four years, and creeping up on forty, I'm pretty damn unemployable by now.

"Lantham?"

I craned my neck back. Saw Jerry and Lynn about ten feet off. He was crouched over her. Hands pressed down on her ass. Looked downright unhappy about it too. They had some decent cover behind a big old redwood stump, thank God.

"Yeah, I'm fine. Peachy." I managed to sit up. Fingers and toes worked. Nothing seemed broken.

The sound of a twelve gauge pump is one of those sounds you can't mistake, even from a ways away. I heard two of them. The bad guys had re-armed. If they had slugs in there, they might be able to punch through our chintzy little cover. "Lynn," I said, "Can you walk?"

"I don't know." She had a tone in her voice that expressed, much better than she could have with any kind of profanity, how utterly undignified she found her predicament. Can't say as I blame her. Being shot is bad enough. Being shot in the ass is worse. It's the one place you can get shot that definitely won't kill you, but you can't sit down for weeks without feeling like somebody spanked you with a rake.

"Give it a try. I'll see what I can do about getting you an ice pack." I wasn't too worried about her, as long as I could get them somewhere a little more secure.

Jerry started to stand up, becaus civilians in a gunfight don't think about things like "the stump is too short to protect me if I stand up."

"Hey! Down!" Now, before you say anything, I know people don't like being ordered around like dogs—except at certain clubs that I'll never admit to my mother that I've even heard of—but...ugh. Civilians. "Jerry. Drop!"

Something in my tone got through to him. He dropped down out of the line of fire. Nobody shot at him—that worried me more than the alternative. It meant they were repositioning. I checked out from my spot—the car was still there, and nobody seemed to be in it.

"Well, ain't that just glorious. We gotta move guys, and we gotta do it now."

I duck-walked across the distance, kept my eyes on the road just above us instead of on the car. That's where I'd be coming if I was them. Either there or down the hill and across—or, better yet, doing both. I'd heard shotgun pumps, they might be moving in for the close kill, more reliable.

You don't have to be accurate with a shotgun to put your man down. You barely have to be sober enough to point the thing straight.

"Come on, Lynn," I took her hand, dragged her to her

feet. I don't think I took her arm out of her socket. "We need to be gone like yesterday."

So we gone-d. Stumbled down hill. Barely managed to stay upright. Through the blackberries, the poison oak, the redwood thickets, and then that last twenty feet, almost straight down to just above that little fire trail we'd been on before.

They got a bead on us a couple times. I heard a bang. Sometimes an impact, never quite in the right place. None of us caught anything metal with our meat.

Somewhere along the line I noticed my ears ringing, pulled the plugs to give them some stimulation, see if I could listen for our pursuit. We picked our way west parallel to that trail, one story up, looking for that granite outcrop. Ran into it pretty damn quick, too.

We crossed the trail leading up to the house, I pulled the civilians into the brush on the far side, behind a deadfall. Tried to keep them on hard ground so there wouldn't be much to track them by. I needed to get the drop on these fuckers or we were pretty much dead.

Behind the deadfall, there was a tall-ish old redwood husk, hollowed out and charred by an ancient forest fire—or maybe a not-so-ancient case of rot-plus-campfire. The kind of thing you find in forests around here that weren't logged to death in the early part of last century. Big enough to stick those two in, and hang out alongside to keep watch.

Lynn wasn't doing too well. The movement was keeping her wounds open. She was bleeding more than I was strictly comfortable with. She might have left enough of a blood trail that hiding wouldn't work in any case.

But the bad guys weren't close. Or, at least, I couldn't hear them out there. Not yet.

"Jerry," I didn't whisper. I just talked low. So low I could barely hear it. Whispers attract attention. They don't carry, not really, but the high frequencies cut through the kind of low rumbling stillness you find in forests like this. You want to keep yourself alive, you get close, you speak low. Almost no breath behind it. "What happened? Why didn't you get out?"

"W...w...we almost made it out to the road. Tried to go up the hill, first, but there was just a barn up there."

"A barn?"

"Y...yeah. L..l...looks like someone had horses."

"Had?"

"Nothing there n...n...now. Just empty space, and some kind of arena..."

"Like a corral?"

"Right. Like that. So we t...t...turn around and head down th..that dirt d...driveway you came up. One of those guys, he was down there watching. He didn't see us. So we hid out, below the driveway, near the wreck. Then s...saw you."

Well, that gave me the geography at least. Nothing I hadn't guessed, but nice to have it confirmed.

"How big was this barn?"

He shrugged. "Barn sized."

Big help, this guy. "Okay, stay quiet. Switch places with me."

He did.

I got in the hollow with Lynn, got her to show me her ass. Needed to see what kind of damage we were talking about.

Wasn't bad. A through-and-through that clipped her right cheek. No real way to bandage it without tape, but it wasn't weeping too much.

"You don't have any gauze on you, do you?" I asked.

"Do I look like a pharmacist?"

"Just thought I'd ask. Here, give me your fingers. This'll hurt a bit." I guided her fingers to the wounds. "Feel that? You need to keep pressure on it. Now, I'm going to leave you here..."

"What? Don't you..."

"Shut up. I'm going to leave you here so I can lure them away. You stay here. I'll get the paramedics here as soon as I can to patch you up."

She liked being told to shut up even less than she liked me telling her I was gonna strand her here. That was nothing next to how much she didn't like what I said next.

"Now, before I go, I need one more thing."

"What's that?"

"Your wallet."

YOU GOTTA RESPECT PEOPLE WHO are good sports. Lynn wasn't, but she was close enough that I was willing to let her skate by like I'm grading on a curve. I figure she deserved credit for making it this far on a day like this. She was going to be fine, at least in the bleed-out department. As long as she kept quiet, she oughta make it out alive.

Me? I figured I'd have a solid win if I made it through the next fifteen or twenty minutes without taking on more lead.

I soft-footed it out of that tree hollow and touched Jerry on the shoulder. He jumped, but didn't yelp.

"You ready?" I talked low—not a whisper, just low enough that I could barely hear what I was saying.

"For what?" He whispered.

I shook my head at him. "Don't whisper, it carries, talk low like this."

"Like this?"

"Just like that. Good." Nice and quiet, like the rest of the forest. Something about all those redwoods, pines, bays, and oaks just eats up sound like they live on it. I kept feeding them, nice and low. "We need to take these guys out of the equation, and I need your help."

I told him what to do, and the two of us pussyfooted like a pair of panthers. Every time one of us clipped a pebble or a twig, hot oil raced up and down my back. I strained, trying to listen to anything that might warn me the bad guys were closing in, maybe knew where we were.

My ears were ringing like someone strapped a vibrator to a church bell. *Ears, Lantham. You're gonna lose your goddamn ears before you hit fifty.* Trying to focus on anything unusual in the background forest fuzz was like trying to spot a leopard in a pile of leaves with bad eyes and no glasses.

Rachael was right: All that unprotected gunfire might just cost me my life.

Forty five seconds, more or less, on the packed dirt path, and we made it to the cobbled grass. Then drew level with the house. I walked with my 1911 pointed down safe, and wished I could afford to pop my ear plugs back in. I pushed an open palm down behind me, hoping Jerry would get the idea to squat low and hold up.

I slunk ahead. Another five seconds. I was even with the road.

Looked around. Didn't see a thing. I waved him forward.

He moved. While he did, I dropped Lynn's wallet. Then, when he was right behind me, the two of us made a dash up the hill to the barn. I dragged my right heel as I did. Deep gouges in the dirt-and-gravel.

Not a barn, so much, as a stable. But it would do.

Little tool shed sticking off one side, no good for hiding in, just a bunch of old paints and thinners, tools and rags, bottles of all kinds. The inside of the stable was more promising.

It had a lobby-area for hanging tack, six stalls, and a central aisle for the horses and hay to go down. Good geography. Twelve feet, up, good solid-looking rafters. The building wasn't all that old, even though the timbers had all gone gray like a beach fence. Probably built by people who didn't want to use chemicals.

Late seventies, maybe. Earlier than that and they would've used pitch, at least in this climate. Later than that, Thompson's or something. But not if a couple hippies had put it together as part of a retreat from the rest of the war-torn world, trying to get back to nature. The house looked like it was built about the same time, made sense to me they'd do it all in one go.

It didn't smell very horsey to me. Whoever owned the place didn't keep any animals up here anymore. The hay on the ground was all flat and half-black in the mud and manure. A ghost of the hay it used to be. Just texture for the thick dirt on the floorboards.

Daylight slanted in through the doors leading out into paddocks. Light shafts like something out of a moody photograph. Lots of contrast. Good for cover.

Not as good as complete darkness, but I'll take what I can get.

I thought about the beams above. Good place to get the drop on somebody, if I could stay balanced through the gunfire, and resist the impulse to duck. On a clear-headed day, that might be a good play. Today, I was rattled enough that I wasn't interested in playing fancy.

Or fair for that matter.

So how do you get a couple professionals to walk into an ambush like rubes?

There's the trick. I took cover in one of the stalls behind the half-tall wall. Whoever built this thing wanted the old timey style, and didn't go in for metal bars or post-and-beam on the stalls. They did proper walls, about three feet high, of tongue-and-groove planks slotted in between two-by-six beams.

Nowhere near thick enough to stop a bullet, but enough of a blind that they wouldn't see me.

Jerry didn't follow me in. He just stood there waiting to be told what to do. Some people shake shell-shock off quick. Some people freeze. This guy was somewhere in the middle. He shook it off enough to take direction, but he couldn't think for himself. Not under fire.

I had to stash him somewhere. I'd meant to use him, but the geography here wasn't good for that. I couldn't have him play bait, these guys were too quick on the trigger. I didn't see anything he could use to club 'em from behind with, we didn't have any sandbags on ropes, and there weren't any goddamn farm tools hanging on the walls.

This place hadn't just gone to seed, it had been cleaned out and left to rot in the fog. You think there'd at least be be something in here for cover when the lead started flying. An old trough, anything that might have a prayer of stopping a ricochet.

Somewhere out there, they were coming for us. The couldn't be far behind now.

And as much as all this was Rachael's fault, I'd forgive her every problem her little stunt caused if I could have her back right now. In all the world, I never met someone I'd rather be shoulder to shoulder with in a gunfight. Not Special Agent Ronald Rivers, not my old partner Alexia Lopez, not even Erica with all her FBI training, much as I love her. They'd all do in a pinch. They'd all be great. But when you go in with Rachael, you know you're coming out alive and on top. Best partner I ever had.

Just don't tell her I said so.

Jerry skittered around the corner and dove into the stall. "Lantham. Lantham!"

"Shut up," I hissed at him.

"But..."

I shot him a look that scared the living fuck out of him. He washed pale, which is a hell of a trick when your skin is that dark.

Then I heard it. A twig breaking. Around the side of the stable. And some footfalls out front. Not close yet. Hard to tell how far away they were, exactly, through the ringing in my ears. Sounded like they were making a full circle. They knew we were in here. So which way would they come in?

Lantham, you idiot, these guys are professionals.

I was thinking like a rube. These guys wouldn't come in at all. They'd just kill us from there.

"Goddammit," I breathed.

"What?"

"Let's hope they need proof-of-death."

"What?"

"How well can you climb?"

"W...W...WHAT DO YOU MEAN by proof of d...death?"

"I'll explain later." I was taking a hell of a risk, but I was out of options. "Can you climb?" I'd laid a trap and forgot to plan for an escape hatch. Now our only chance was that they really were professionals.

If they didn't, we were as good as dead.

"Yeah. I c...c...can."

"Good." Professionals will have to prove they did the job. Usually that means they'd take a head or a hand to show to the client. And they'll want to get away as clean as possible, without attracting attention. So they weren't going to torch the place with us inside it. Times like this, when you place your bet with your own personal skin, you need a hell of a poker face. "I'll boost you."

We weren't small guys. Jerry wasn't as tall as I was but he made up for it by being a code monkey and a bit older. Five seconds later, he was wedged between that beam and the ceiling. I told him to keep his arms and legs above the wood, which he could only do by pushing against the ceiling and sitting Indian-style.

It wasn't until he was up there that I noticed the flaw in my logic. They wouldn't torch the place with us inside it...

...unless they wanted to drive us out onto open ground.

So our only prayer was that they didn't want to risk attracting attention from the fire department, which they had to know was gonna come for those burning cars before too long.

But if they didn't torch the place, they were gonna Swiss cheese the hell out of it.

Jerry in place, I rolled out of the stall, fast-crept along till I was even with the next pair of stall doors—staying low enough that they wouldn't be able to catch the movement through the windows—and under the next big rafter. Second exposed beam of the three in the place, about dead center in the building. I peeked up, looked both ways before crossing the line of fire just like my dear old Mom told me to do, then jumped and wrapped both arms around the beam.

Big mistake. My left arm just plain didn't want to flex that way, and it marshaled a legion of flamethrowers and aimed them at my nerve endings. That made me grunt, and louder than I meant to.

I clamped down with my right, and swung my feet up. My heels caught around the beam just as the walls exploded, spitting splinters everywhere.

Loud. The gunmen were right outside those walls. They made a gazebo out of the place, and filled it with toothpicks besides. Slugs whizzed through like little F-16s, and I was sure I was gonna wind up with some new holes before I got my bearings.

I scrambled and swung and got myself up on top of that beam. I could only get to my 1911. I pulled it, checked the load. Four rounds left in the mag, plus the one in the pipe. Five shots.

Looked to Jerry. He was trying to hold his ears between his arms. Trying not to scream.

I managed to get my earplugs back in, for all the good it'd do me. Felt like I was listening to the world sing a one-note tune with bad percussion on the other side of a wall made of pillows.

They were carrying a lot of bullets. A goddamn awful lot of bullets. Not just handgun rounds either. They'd been carrying some hefty hardware in that trunk. I could hear an AR-15. Little .223 slugs that packed a hell of a lot of punch. They ripped through both sides of that stable like it was made of wet toilet paper. Now that the lead was flying, I could see where the guys out there were coming from.

One out front, another on the downhill side, firing up. Way *too* up for my taste. He was trying to fire flat in order to hit people in there on the ground. Neither of them had thought to shoot for the rafters. But even so, I had little angry bees zipping past me every time he lost control of his recoil.

I was tempted to try to shoot back through the wood at him, but without a bead I'd be wasting my ammo, and I didn't have a lot left to go around. My mother said I never could learn from my own mistakes, but she's wrong. I remember how much embarrassment I suffered as an overeager teenager, so I held my wad.

Now, the real gamble:

Were they going to keep on firing until they ran dry? Or were they going to come in and investigate? Were they waiting for a telltale groan and scream? Or was there some kind of method, where they were sectioning the whole building and would come in once they were sure that nobody could possibly have survived?

Well, it couldn't be the latter. I had no reason to think they'd been in here yet, and every reason to think otherwise, so they couldn't know for sure that there wasn't good cover in here. If I was them, I'd take a good methodical sweep through, reposition, and go again, if I had the ammo. If I didn't, I'd stretch out the assault, wait for someone to scream, and then either come in careful-like, or camp out and wait for someone to talk or stumble out, anything that'd let me get a good, clear, unambiguous shot at them.

Come on, Lantham. Pull something out of your ass. Come up with something quick.

So I did. I screamed.

Jerry just about fell off his perch. Looked at me like I was completely nuts.

It worked. The gunshots stopped.

Not that I could hear anything else after all that racket. Best I could do was hunch up and press myself back against the ceiling.

I saw a shadow in the paddock off a stall across the way and toward the front.

Then some thumping, like the door on that shed. If I got lucky, I might be able to catch him shooting blind through the wall. I started repositioning so I could get a steady shot, but before I finished there was more thumping, like the door had gone closed.

Then I saw shoes. This guy was going to come straight through where he had an eyeline on me and Jerry. I was going to have to shut him up or put him down, but if I used the gun, the sound would make the other guy drop back and set up to pick us off when we left here, like we'd eventually have to. Then I'd have to call the cops again and hope they got up here before he figured out some other angle on how to drive us out—like torching the place.

But Mr. Shoes wasn't coming in. He was doing something else.

He was flipping open a Zippo. Guess he had the same idea I did.

He knew we were in here now. He knew that at least one of us wasn't dead. He was going to smoke us out.

Jerry's eyes were wide. Bright white saucers of terror in his deep-dark face, with black holes in the middle big enough to swallow galaxies. He'd figured it out too.

We were in a tinderbox, and once the fire really caught, we'd have a couple minutes, tops, to get out of here.

A bottle came through the paddock door.

Spinning in the air.

With a streak of orange behind it.

All the exits were covered. The guy in front would

have the uphill paddocks under bead. Mr. Shoes would keep his side covered nice and tight.

The bottle hit.

It shattered.

Liquid fire splashed across the middle of the building.

I had two seconds, maybe less.

My 1911 took a good look at Mr. Shoes. It's muzzle tilted up by a few degrees. Gut shot. Dead center mass.

I squeezed.

Mr. Shoes stumbled back. I didn't wait for him to recover his balance. I followed it up with two more, one to the gut, and one a little higher. Headshot, I hoped. Full Mozambique. Efficient. Lucky that he was at just the right distance for it.

One down. One to go.

I hit the floor before the flames hit the ceiling. I held my finger to my lips and looked at Jerry, still frozen up there on his roasting rack.

Come on, get down, you idiot. I waved my arms like a drunk chicken.

He held on too long. Long enough that I couldn't be sure anymore that we had a good escape.

Long enough that I was having trouble breathing.

The smoke is what pushed him down. That first lungful, wrapping his body around that much no-oxygen, coughing like a chain smoker with TB. He knocked himself right off that rafter, managed to half-catch it on the way down, enough to land feet first instead of head-first.

He was on the other side of the fire, and the fire was

making itself right at home.

I took a running start, stomped through it, got my hands on him, dragged him back through the other side. Get the fire between us and the bad guy. Give us two escape routes.

Figure out where the fuck he was.

"Stay low," I told him. "Take your shirt off. Breathe through it. Lay down and don't get up until we run for it, unless the fire gets here."

Then I rolled out to the side door of the back paddock on the downhill side. I didn't have my dental mirror with me—I wasn't expecting to need it, and I only take it along on snoop jobs on account of I don't like walking around like a fully stocked spy shop if I don't need to.

I was trying to get air out of a thick soup of black I couldn't seen through. The stable smelled like a campfire, looked like a coal cloud, and sounded like all hell got crammed into a closet. Less than two minutes into the fire, and it was so hot that if either of us stood up, we'd flash-cook. I didn't have time for half measures anymore, which is what they'd been counting on.

First I looked around from inside the paddock door. Didn't see anything. Looked fast, but looked close.

He hadn't moved into line-of-sight here. Was he still covering from the front?

I took one of the burner phones—a term that, considering my current predicament, I was not fond of—and used the screen as a mirror to peer around the corner. Had to make it quick. Had to pray to hell that I didn't accidentally flash the sun at him and give my position away.

Checked the sun position. Made sure I wouldn't bounce the light wrong. I still had a thin finger of shade from the pre-noon sun. Thank God for slim chances.

I scanned, best I could. Didn't see him.

Looked close. Moved slow as I dared. Just to make sure that he wasn't propped next to a tree or laying prone in the brush near the road.

But he wouldn't would he? He'd be on the move, pacing back and forth, waiting for the cattle to stampede, making sure they didn't get out.

Now I was the one stuck in freeze-mode.

I had no good options. If I rolled through that door, he might get me from any angle. If I didn't, I was smoked duck, and overcooked besides.

Three seconds. That's about all I had.

But I didn't see him. I really didn't. So I took the gamble. I stuck my gun out the door first.

Then my head.

Then I scooted until I was all the way out, still lying prone.

I reached down into my pocket with my left, got the revolver. I might need a quick iron-swap.

The smoke licked out the doorway above me like someone was pouring oil into the sky. I needed to wave Jerry out, but I needed to be able to spot a clearing first.

I checked back at him. He was laying there, still alive. Still conscious. Belly pressed into the dirt-and-hay. Naked from the waist up. His short-sleeve button-up clutched to his face with both arms for all he was worth.

Breathing was his big task.

On the far side, the smoke poured out the opposite paddock. The air in between the ground and the flames and the smoke was oily and wiggly, like someone had turned the atmosphere into a lava lamp.

A motion attracted my eye. The figure of the other gunman held it. I swung over, drew a bead. Jerry , if you want to keep breathing, don't you fucking move.

Bang bang.

Bad guy goes down.

"Jerry, get over here, now. Out of there."

He didn't move. His back was starting to blister. The flames were creeping towards his face. I couldn't tell if it was too hot in there for him to move, or too loud for him to hear, or too scary for him to know what the fuck was going on,

Goddammit.

I dove back in. Had to slide on my stomach.

It was like sticking your face in a pizza oven. Any second, my whiskers would going to catch on fire and my eyebrows would flash-evaporate.

My fingers found him. Dug into his arms.

I hauled him back.

Couldn't keep my eyes open. My eyeballs would poach.

He scrabbled with his legs.

Between the two of us we got him out of the fireplace and onto the hearth.

Soon as we were clear, and coughing up our lungs, I

dragged him to his feet.

"Go back to Lynn. Fast as you can. Go, go. I'll meet you there."

He nodded dumbly, climbed over the paddock railing, dropped into the undergrowth on the downhill side.

I caught my breath. Running on nothing more than instinct now. I had to make sure these assholes were dead.

The guy on this side was still twitching. The third shot had clipped his throat, shattered his jaw. He'd bleed out, but it would take a while. He was flapping his hand against the ground, trying to reach his gun, but it was out past his fingers, and he couldn't turn his head to see where to reach.

The paddock floor was starting to get a bit muddy from the blood, and his shoes were melting in the heat.

I stepped over him and kicked the gun away. It skittered off the poured pad and into the poison oak on the hillside. For just a second, the part of me that hates seeing dogs flopping around after they get hit by a car considered popping him in the prefrontal. Just to put him out of his misery. It would be the humane thing to do.

But I wasn't feeling very humane.

I also didn't want to have to try to explain that kind of move to the DA. They frown on that. And this jerk wasn't worth going to the slammer for.

And if I stayed here much longer I was gonna roast. My back was slick-wet with sweat from the heat. It felt like every inch of me was breaking out in blisters.

I left the almost-corpse to roast, made like a frog and leaped over the rail, hopped across to the drive. Hooked a right around the front of the used-to-be-a-stable, headed up into the corral so I had good coverage on the other paddock.

Well, I had to check the other guy. If he was alive enough to be worth the bother, I might be able to get some answers out of him.

Got proud of the rails where I could see in. I knew I'd dropped the guy in the left hand paddock.

Trouble was, the only thing I saw there was a mess of roasting dirt.

11:55 AM, THURSDAY

THAT BARN WAS BURNING SO hot now I could barely stand to be twenty feet from it. The trees leaning in overhead were going to catch pretty damn quick, and then this whole hillside would go up like tinder. Redwood and pine burn like they're filled with turpentine, because they actually are.

Not a lot of minutes left before I had to be running my ass off just make sure I lived to screw up another day.

But I had a few. And this bozo was not going to give me the slip, not if I had anything to say about it.

I tried to get closer, see if I could track him, but that was a loser of a plan. Even three feet closer made me feel like my face was gonna melt off.

Truth to tell, it probably would have if I got much closer than that.

But that meant the gunman couldn't be much closer to the fire than me, and he couldn't have gone far. I checked around to make sure that I wasn't on the wrong end of a gun, then peered into the paddock, seeing if I could spot a trail.

No dice.

But if I was him, I'd either have hot-footed it up here to the corral, or I'd have headed down the hill.

Why he hadn't tried to shoot me again I couldn't guess, unless I'd managed to lame his trigger arm.

I ran back down to the drive, scanning the dirt in front of me.

There you are you sneaky bastard.

Blood. A healthy amount of it. I'd winged him, for sure.

I followed the trail quick as I could. If he was still armed—and he sure as hell hadn't left his AR-15 down in the paddock—then he might still go after Jerry.

And Jerry was headed straight back to Lynn.

I sped up. One foot in front of the other, running down the hill like a good little lemming.

When I got to the fork, where the driveway met the trail leading down to the granite outcrop, and right past where Lynn was hiding, the blood went left.

Right towards Jerry and Lynn.

Any sane mercenary would head back to the car, regroup, plan the hit for later. This guy was seriously motivated.

What the hell do these people know that an entire hit team would be willing to die to put them out of commission?

I was about to find out. I swapped out the .45—which only had one or two rounds left in it—for the .357.

At this point, I wasn't too worried about being heard. This guy left me a trail every bit as clear as if he'd been spraying paint at the ground. He was losing enough blood that I didn't expect him to still be standing for very long—I just couldn't take the chance that he'd get a few shots off before he keeled over.

Up ahead, to the left of the trail, I heard a ruckus. Someone struggling.

Thrashing in the underbrush.

Grunting. A woman's voice.

And a man's.

A crack. The kind of crack you hear when someone gets whacked on the noggin hard enough to kill them.

And then a crumple on the forest carpet.

And that moaning. Moaning that makes you remember every single headache you've ever had. Makes you afraid to wake up tomorrow, just in case you get a migraine like that.

I got to the site of the noise in time to see Lynn standing over the dying gunman, and holding the AR-15 on Jerry, who was bleeding from a cut on his forehead and groaning in agony.

Lynn was shaking like a robin chick in a snow storm.

"Lynn! Don't do it!" I was close enough to hit her with that little revolver. Not close enough to be sure I'd only wing her. "I've killed two people today. Don't make it three."

"I have to." She said it like she was trying to convince herself.

"Drop it, Lynn." Jerry was writhing on the ground, holding his head, curling up in a fetal position. Looked like a massive, uncontrollable ball of pain. I shuffled forward, tried to get close enough. If I could just get close enough...

"I can't!" Another couple steps. Still a good fifteen feet away.

"Why can't you?" Two more steps. Almost lunging distance. Her body was facing toward me, though. And her finger was on the trigger. If I hit her like a football player, that trigger finger might squeeze, and Jerry would get a new cooling duct.

"I...I..." She gritted her teeth. Pressed her lips together in a fine line. You can see determination coming over someone who's never killed before. That moment when they walk across that narrow bridge from "normal person" to "killer."

Lynn was crossing that bridge.

Her finger twitched.

"Don't do it, Lynn, don't you fucking do it. You don't want to die here. You don't want to go to jail..."

"I'm sorry."

She bore down. Just a little shift of her weight. Bracing herself against recoil.

Aw, fuck.

I was just close enough.

I flicked my wrist.

The little revolver sailed end-over end at her head.

She caught the motion, turned to see what it was. The rifle dropped off target.

The revolver smashed into her eye. Heavy thing like that, even just lobbed softly, it's enough to knock most people over.

Lynn didn't disappoint me. She fell back. The rifle went off, the slug went into the ground, and Lynn went onto her back.

I ran in right behind, got the rifle out of her hands. Picked up the revolver.

Now I had two civvies rolling around on the ground crying and clutching their heads.

Fuck 'em anyway.

I checked the gunman. Bleeding out, bad. Already unconcsious, but not quite dead yet.

Judging by the holes I'd punched in him, he had to be bleeding into his gut. Long slow awful way to die.

"Hey." I squatted down beside him. "How's it going?"

He bled at me. Well, coughed, really. But there was a lot of blood that came out with the air.

"Who hired you?"

"Fuck you."

I reached a balled fist out, pressed it gently on his stomach. "I don't want to be an asshole, but you've kind of ruined my morning." I spoke slowly, kinda friendly, like you'd talk to a rabid dog while you're reaching for a rock. "The medics are on their way, and they might be able to save you if you last that long. So I'm going to make this really simple." I leaned on him a little more. He moaned. The kind of low pathetic moan you make when you can't scream, because it hurts too much. "Tell me who hired you. Who's paying the bills?"

He coughed.

Moaned.

Rattled.

I pulled out my pre-paid. "I'll call the corpsmen right now. Get them up here. They're already on the way. They might already be down at the car crash right now. I'll just tell them to send the ambulance up the driveway to the fire. They'll be here in five minutes."

"Okay, man. Okay, okay, okay..." he trailed off.

I leaned down, so I'd be close enough to hear.

"Boswell, man." He barely managed a whisper. "Boswell called the job..." He ran out of air, grabbed for some more, but it all came out in coughs, then in strawberry foam.

"Who's Boswell?"

He gurgled at me.

"Goddammit, who's Boswell?" I shouted to get through the pain fog, but this guy was rounding the bend at "mostly dead" and racing full-bore for "all dead." His body was hanging on, but it wasn't doing its job of keeping his brain alive. It was worried about twitching and flopping like a fish.

I punched him in the gut wound. He'd die faster, but he'd be more awake, and he could fucking well deal with the suffering. Lynn and Jerry were still nursing their head wounds, and this guy was trying to die on me without giving me any answers.

"They..." cough "...they don't say. It's just orders. Just orders."

I punched him again. This time he yowled loud, the kind of yowl you hear from a dying elephant. Turns your heart to ice and wraps your guts up in knots. That yowl scared deer out of the brush a dozen yards off to the left.

The gunman's stomach gave around my fist. He seized, went into convulsions.

Then he wet himself.

And then he didn't do much of anything. His leg twitched against me once or twice, but that was it.

I'd had all I was going to take of this shit. My body decided it was done with me, and I lunged to the side and puked my guts out.

SANTA CRUZ AND SAN MATEO COUNTY have some of the best forests on the planet. They all smell like heaven, with the salt fog, and the redwoods, and the bay trees. It smells clean in a way you don't get most other places. Even when it's starting to fill with smoke from the fire up the hill, it smells clean.

It smells like the kind of place you can have a good day.

I had my face pressed down into the dirt, sucking the loamy earthy healthy smell up into my nostrils like it could unmake this morning. Like it could stop me from getting up and taking this job, or from using that first guy as a human shield, or doing a messy kill on that second guy, leaving him to bleed out with his jaw off, or torturing this last fucker to death. I'd added a pile of hurt to the world today, and for no good reason at all as far as I could tell. Just cause I was in the wrong place at the wrong time. Just cause I was pissed that they killed my car. Just because I was protecting these two bozos who were too naïve to live, far as I could tell.

Doc Samson's gonna be happy with all these new issues I've

*broken out in. Asshole's gonna make a fortune off the therapy
sessions.*

I wondered if Klepto would be able to tell when I got
home. If he'd smell the death on me and decide I wasn't a
good guy anymore. If he'd run away to find some decent
person to make his meals and scratch his ears and loan
him a pillow.

There's a thing about violence. A thing you learn the
hard way:

You can get used to it, and think you can handle it, but
if you run into a new kind, you're a greeny all over again.
Shooting someone shakes you up the first time. After that
it gets easier. But if you have to go after someone with a
knife, or your fists, it's a whole other ballgame. Your body
doesn't know how to deal with it.

Like mine didn't now. Death *this* messy was something
I've only read about.

The civvies had stopped with the moaning. I was still
trying to quiet my gut, but I had to stand up and be the
adult in this situation.

Even though my hand was covered with that guy's
blood.

So I stood. I swooned a little bit. There was a bay tree
a few feet away, in the opposite direction from Jerry and
Lynn, so I stepped over the corpse and made like I was
stretching my legs and collecting my thoughts.

How you can collect something that's burst into a
billion pieces and skittered like marbles down a storm
drain, I don't know, but I did what I could to collect them
anyway.

The bay tree helped. I leaned on the aligator-skin bark and plucked a couple of the long narrow leaves, and crushed them. They crunched in my hand, and I pressed them up under my nose and breathed them in.

They burned, but only a little. That smell, like something between menthol and an Italian restaurant, brought my floaty brain right back down to earth all nice and solid. Like breathing could flush the adrenaline and euphoria out of my system. Grounding, that's what it was.

Also tamped down the nausea and kept me from trying to vomit up my own kidneys, which was nice.

I didn't get so much as a word out before Lynn started swearing at me. I learned things about my family history in the first ten seconds that would've astonished my mother and every dog I ever owned. And, to be honest, I wasn't up for genealogy just now. Or bullshit. So I tromped back across the ground, over the body, and to where Lynn was half-standing, and grabbed her by the hair.

Not my most diplomatic moment, but, then, it wasn't my best morning in recent memory either.

She screamed. I lifted. Got her to where she was up on her toes and out at arm's length.

Her hair wasn't bearing her weight, but it hurt her enough that she stayed right up on her toes and tried like hell to beat my arm into letting her go. I was tempted to do just that, and let her fall right on her ass where she'd get a reminder the hard way that she'd been shot not too long ago.

"Why were you trying to kill Jerry?"

"Ow! Ow. They made me!"

"Who?"

"You have to let me go. They're going to kill him."

"Who?"

"Yeah, I'd like to know too, *partner.*" Jerry spat the whole sentence out. He was still laying on the ground clutching his head. She'd given him a hell of a crack. I was guessing she did it with the butt of the rifle.

"Deck. My husband. He's...ow...they're going to kill him."

I let her down a little—not enough that she could get loose, just enough that she could stand flat-footed. I kept just as tight a hold on her hair. Not hard, since I'm as tall as a bungalow and I've got hands like an excavator.

Gave me something to concentrate on that wasn't dead, too. That was a plus.

"They're going to kill him. Who's 'they'?"

"I don't know. I...when we were down at Loma Mar this morning, I went out to go to the bathroom, and someone in the next stall started talking. She said they had my husband, and they were going to kill him. She handed me this fob and told me to put it on my key ring. She said to hit the unlock button when we passed this one sign on the road. The one that says falling rocks?"

They made her trigger the bomb that sent her off the road? Or did they just get her to warn them when the Jeep was in ambush position?

"Who was she?"

"I don't know. I didn't see her."

"So you just left and didn't tell anyone." Lynn was a

lot of things, but I couldn't believe she was that stupid.

"Of course not."

"So what happened?"

"I got a message before I could tell anyone. A picture. Deck. From this morning. It said 'Keep your mouth shut.'"

"And you don't know who it is?"

"No."

"Do you know where your husband is?"

"He's at work. Works at Kepler's."

"Glamorous."

"Fuck you."

I let her go. "Have a seat."

She didn't sit.

So I stepped right up to her and loomed, and shouted. "*Sit down.*"

Lovely thing, looming. A looming Lantham lays 'em low, laconic and lasting, like liquor. She sat.

And remembered her bullet wound the hard way.

"Now stay there and shut up."

I stepped back and retrieved the rifle, just so she didn't get any ideas, and slung it over my shoulder. I figured the corpse was armed too, but I wasn't interested in frisking it for weapons at the moment, so I just stood in between it and her so she couldn't get to it without going through me.

Then I pulled out my pre-paid and checked for signal. I had some. I gave Cal a call.

"Cal," Cal said.

"Hey, it's Lantham. We got a forest fire going up here.

We're going to need a fire copter."

"What?"

"Just...it's a long story. I've got three dead bad guys, three wrecked cars, to of them on fire, two injured civilians, one forest fire, a load of buckshot in my left arm..."

"...and a partridge in a pear tree."

"Hmph. At this point, I'd believe anything. Look, just watch for the bonfire in the gully by the side of the road, then come up the dirt driveway just east of there on the south side. In about a hundred fifty yards, you'll get to this blue-trimmed hippie cabin with a trail leading downhill on its west side. Follow the trail down, you'll find me camped there with the civilians."

"What about the fire?"

Good question. I looked back in that direction. I could smell a little smoke, but not a hell of a lot. Looked like it was mostly headed up hill, being blown east by the coastal winds. We were due north, and downhill besides, so we were probably okay for the moment.

"I think we're safe for now, but I've got an escape route if that changes. How far out are you?"

"Any minute now."

"Great. One more thing. You got a radio in that car of yours?"

"I do."

"Get a bunch of units out to Kepler's in Palo Alto. There's a guy there by the name of Deck...What's his last name?" I asked Lynn.

"Fraiser."

"Deck Fraiser. He works there. He's being used as leverage against these civvies. I'm betting the fourth member of the hit team is there in the store. Get 'em in there and save his life before the bad guys start wondering why their buddies haven't called in the all clear yet?"

"Jesus, Lantham, what've you gotten into?"

"You tell me, buddy, I just work here."

"I'll be there as soon as I can."

"Thanks. I'll keep the phone handy."

Cal rang off. I checked the phone, make sure I hadn't missed anything important in all the fire and gunfire excitement. No incoming calls, no missed messages. If Earl hadn't called back yet, he must've fallen down a rabbit hole. That might mean this whole business with their company was a lot more complicated than they made it sound.

"Cops are going to pick up your husband. You can relax."

She did. Visibly. For the first time since I met her, she didn't look like a cornered wolf sizing up a hiker.

I sat down cross-legged on the soft forest carpet. Didn't realize how completely beat I was till my ass hit the ground.

"Okay, let's try this again. Someone's trying to kill you. Someone really wants you dead. Someone rich, and powerful, and who doesn't mind burning down San Mateo county to do it. And that someone also targeted you when you were meeting with Gus Ferris at Camp Loma Mar..."

"How do you know..." Lynn said, but I wasn't gonna

let her interrupt me till I got the whole thought out, because I wasn't too keen on my ability to keep my thoughts all herded together right now.

"I know a lot things. Like this: I know that you're both as good as dead, cause if these guys didn't work, the next team will.

"Now. We've got about five minutes to figure out who this might be, before the cops get here. So I want you both, as quick as you can, to explain everything I might possibly need to know about the blockchain and what the hell an identity brokerage is."

Jerry started. Lynn filled in, translating the geek-speak more than I really needed. But I didn't care.

Cause what they told me scared the ever-loving fuck out of me.

TURNS OUT THE ONE THING THAT makes digital currencies like Bitcoin work is a little computing trick called "the blockchain." It's a kind of distributed spreadsheet. Everybody has a full copy, all the reads and writes occur simultaneously and in public, it can't be controlled by any central authority. Using the blockchain, you can have actual digital do-dads—unique bits of data that can't be copied—not like "it's copy-protected and the computer won't let you do it without hacking the crypto key," but it flat can't be copied. It can only be transferred.

Think of all those science fiction movies that have some plot point that rely on people stealing files, where the victim of the theft finds out about it because the files are missing, like they would be if someone took a paper file.

People who live in Internet-land, like I've wound up doing as a byproduct of growing up in Silicon Valley, tend to roll our eyes at scenes like this. A file on a computer isn't a *thing*, it's a *representation* of a thing. It's an idea, an abstraction. It's a description, and it can be copied any time its read. In order to have a computer file act like it does in science fiction movies, it would have to be what philosophers call a "thing-in-itself."

So, yeah, we tend to think scenes like that were pretty stupid. Or we did until Bitcoin came around. Suddenly, now there was a kind of file that was a thing-in-itself. A real digital analog of a physical thing. It takes real resources to create it, and it can't be copied.

It sounded neat, and any hacker or computer geek worth his gonads played around with buying, selling, or mining a few in the early years. But the thing that missed most of us, the thing that missed me, is that the big deal about Bitcoin wasn't the idea of money that didn't depend on a government or a bank.

The big deal with Bitcoin is that it made digital files into *things*. It was possible to have a unique thing in cyberspace. Each Bitcoin has a serial number. It can be subdivided, but it can't be duplicated. Each one has a *selfness* about it, the same way that a hand-carved chess piece does.

So, I thought when Jerry got to this point, *you can make collectibles and prevent piracy using this trick, and without doing things that piss off your customers. Movie studios everywhere will be proud.*

Because, as Jerry then pointed out, I was missing the big picture. The blockchain—that bit that makes Bitcoins work—makes digital *things*. A digital *thing*, that can't be counterfeited and can't be duplicated, even in theory, means that you can finally have *things* like digital signatures, or digital title deeds, or digital records.

Or digital identities.

You can make an entire trustworthy economy with it. From cash that holds its value and can't be diluted, to title deeds that can't be faked or fraudulent, to artificial people that can transact business and be bought or sold like trading cards, because they are, after all, just a file.

It's anonymous, and it's self-governing, and it's entirely self-generating.

That's when I got scared.

Because, if you used microscopic print, the list of people who might want to put a stop to that would be about eighty-three times as long as my arm. This little bitty computing trick could do to governments, property, and the digital economy what Amazon did to publishing and what Wikipedia did to the Trivial Pursuit dispute-settling business. It would do to all of them what the automobile did to the horse industry. What the steam engine did to manufacturing.

Up till now, everything I'd ever read about Bitcoin was about money. These people were taking the underlying tech—which was completely open and usable by anyone—and using it to turn the world on its head. They were mining and getting ready to sell digital identities. And they were planning to sell digital property deeds right behind it. It was all in the plans.

"We're fucked," I said. "There isn't a government or big corporation on this planet that wouldn't have at least one person somewhere in it willing to kill to keep this from hitting the market."

Lynn raised a very cynical eyebrow at me. "We figured that out."

"So who knows about this?"

Jerry shrugged. "A dozen people? Maybe two? We've managed to get by without funding so far. We were going to our first pitch this afternoon, with Palmer's guy."

"Well, that narrows the pool a little. That's somewhere to start. You want me to track these bastards down?"

Lynn nodded. "If you'd please..."

My pocket buzzed. I pulled the phone. "Hey Cal."

"Lantham, I'm at the house. You better get up here if you want a ride out. That fire's getting nasty."

"On our way. Got the coroner handy?"

"He's still twenty minutes out."

"He's gonna find ashes. Want pictures of the body I've got here?"

"Fuck. I better come down."

"Hang a right at the cinderblock flagstones."

Cal's car rolled down the hill a couple minutes later. The civvies climbed in while I gave him a tour of the corpse. Didn't mention Boswell, cause I didn't know what it meant.

He took some pictures for his report, confiscated the rifle, and then we got the hell out of there.

Once we were clear of the woods and down near the road, he pulled over behind a proper police car. They'd attracted quite a crowd. Paramedics were here, and I got shoved in front of them under protest. They took a look at the shotgun blast in my arm and then tortured me for a while cleaning it up and bandaging it before they reluctantly decided that I didn't particularly need to go to the hospital.

As soon as they weren't fussing over me, Cal pulled me aside.

"Do you still have that envelope?"

"Not on me, but yeah."

"Good. Get it to him." He pressed the keys in my hand.

"Where? Why, for fucks sake? You've gotta book me. After an incident like this? They'll have your badge, Cal. I'll spend a night in the cooler and my lawyer will spring me. I know the drill."

"This is too important."

"What is it?"

"I can't tell you that. But you can't let any of these guys find it. If you go to the cooler, they'll find it in inventory."

"Cal, what the hell..."

"Just trust me, Clarke. Please. It's a life and death thing."

Oh, great, another one. "Fine, fine. And how do I get past this retinue of street soldiers in your car? I have to go that way."

"No, you missed that window. Head back over the hill. You know where Ellison's house is, up on the hill in Woodside?"

"Yeah." Larry Ellison, founder of Oracle, had a house up there that made most castles look like fishing shacks. "Who could miss it?"

"Pull into the driveway after his. Look for an old maroon Buick with tinted windows. Make the hand off, then go grab a rental. Tell me where to pick up the car."

"Christ, Cal, I didn't go into the snoop business to turn into a spy." I held up my hands to stop him from cajoling me a second time. "Fine, fine, just...get them all looking the other way for a few minutes."

"You got it."

Cal was as good as his word. He led a team of cops down to check out the scene of the crime, leaving just us chickens up with the paramedics.

I jogged across the road to that tree I'd been hiding behind, found the pack I'd dropped with all the salvage from the cars, then slipped into Cal's car and high-tailed it up the hill.

I SHIT YOU NOT, IF I had any chance to get to a coffee shop between the crash site and the handoff site, I would have opened that envelope and photographed the contents before re-sealing it, and nobody would have been the wiser. The only reason I didn't was the nearest coffee shop was a full five miles past the handoff point, and in this neck of the woods that would have delayed my arrival at the meet by half an hour or an hour.

I know. I checked. Had to call Nya to do it, cause the cheap pre-paid phone wasn't getting any decent data reception.

That kind of delay would've been noticed, and I really didn't want to be holding this particular hot potato when the next group of guys with guns showed up.

So I made the handoff, like Cal asked. Cloak and dagger shit. I didn't even see the man's face. He just rolled down a tinted window and held out his hand. I passed it across. Then I left.

The whole time, something was eating at the back of my brain. Couldn't figure out what it was. It just wouldn't leave me alone.

Met up with the freeway, didn't have to deal with too much mid-day traffic heading down to the San Jose airport. I dropped Cal's car in short term parking, locked the ticket and keys in the car, texted him the space number. Headed in to the Dollar desk and picked myself up a wussy little econo-mobile because I wasn't inclined to drop cash on anything I didn't need to.

On my way out of the airport, that feeling got worse. That brain-gnawing. The kind that tells me I missed something.

Lantham, you idiot, you've got two civvies heading into the hospital and they've still got people after them.

Had to be. Dammit.

"Cal, this is Lantham."

"What's wrong?"

"Make my day and tell me you're smarter than me."

"Done. You're an idiot. What's up?" Any doubts I had about him being Rachael's father ran away and hid every time he opened his mouth.

"Tell me you've got those two in protective custody."

"With a hit team after them? What do you think I am, thick?"

"Thanks. Keep me posted on where they wind up?"

"Oh, they'll be in intensive care at Stanford-UCSF for the rest of the day, I think. We got the husband, too. Safe and sound."

"Great. Thanks. Any suspects there?"

"Nothing. We checked the phones of all the patrons. No one lawyered up, nothing suspicious. Whoever was sitting on him did it from outside the store and bugged out when we got there."

"Tell me you're combing the cameras."

"Yes, Lantham, we're combing the cameras. I'll tell you once we make an arrest, assuming we find anyone. You can come in tomorrow to my office and give a statement?"

He said it like it was a question, because he doesn't need to be rude when he knows I know that he can haul my ass into jail if I say no. "Yeah. I'll be down around lunchtime."

"Make it after lunch. Two o'clock."

Which'll put me right in the middle of rush hour traffic heading home. "Sure. Thanks Cal." Thanks loads, buddy.

"Don't mention it." He had a smirk in his voice when he rang off. Figures.

Oh well, there were two less things to worry about.

Me? I headed home. I needed to do some research, and get my hands on Earl's report. See if I could figure out who was behind this mess—or, failing that, figure out some way to make my clients bullet-proof.

Or, at least, bullet-resistant.

SINCE I DIDN'T HAVE MY old reliable phone working, I had to make do with the pre-paid, which meant I didn't have any of my contacts or toys in there, and I didn't do a hell of a lot of dialing on the way up 880.

But Earl didn't call me back either. Nya did. I put her on speaker and told her I was on my way home. She promised to have some food waiting for me, which normally I'd have objected to in the strongest sense, on the ground that she can't cook for beans, but at this point I was hungry enough to eat bison on the hoof and in the hide.

But Nya had better ideas. I found out about them when I got home.

I parked on the street so I wouldn't box Nya in, and because I didn't want my neighbors thinking I'd willingly possess a Chevy Spark. I came in the front door—not my usual entrance route, so when I slid my key in the lock I heard the surprised, earth-rumbling "woof" of the world's most ridiculous mutt.

Ever wonder what happens when you cross a pit bull and a mastiff? Well, whatever it is, it smiles like the sunrise, slobbers like Niagara falls, and knocks over men who are tall enough to frighten the Eiffel Tower. And that's when it's being friendly.

Sir Klepto the Maniac, the hellhound in question, crested the staircase at the back of the house and rounded the corner, barreling at me on scrambling gangly teenage puppy legs that didn't quite want to stay where he put them.

"Stop!" I snapped and held an open palm out to him. I've been trying to civilize the mutt, since he's now officially big enough to accidentally knock the house over if he turns the wrong way. He's supposed to come to a screeching halt, sit down, and await instructions.

Instead, he skittered to a halt right before he leapt up to knock me over, then stood there twisting his head, first one way, then another, trying to figure out what the hell I was up to.

Lantham, have you forgotten the whole welcome ritual? He seemed to say with those unbelievably huge, confused eyes.

"Sorry, boy, I don't want you bumping my arm. Sit." I snapped again. This one he understood. He planted his ass on the carpet and waited for his reward. "Good boy. Good boy." I ruffled his hair, or what would have been his hair if he was a five year old kid instead of a six month old mutt.

Normally this would be enough to make me happy even after the worst kind of day, but it wasn't Klepto that caught the bulk of my attention. It was the white plastic shopping bag on the coffee table, and the little styrofoam clamshell box inside, with its companion cup-sized styrofoam container filled with Greek salad.

The smell was enough to make me hungry all over again, which made me start rattling. I hadn't eaten since the coffee shop this morning, and none of that food had made it out of the forest alive. I was still none-too-steady on my feet. Figured I'd be rattled for a few days.

Bad business, all that violence. Not good for my mental health. Or anyone else's, for that matter. Might need to take a sleeping pill tonight, so I wouldn't wake up from the nightmares.

Maybe I wasn't hungry after all.

But Klepto hadn't touched the food sitting right there at snout height, which was a hell of a good job for him, especially considering that it smelled like beef, garlic, and a whole lot of heaven.

Nya'd decided to spare me the purgatory of her cooking and order me up some kebabs and a Coke from Villa Roma. Best Greek-style kebabs in the whole East Bay, and they're sold from a pizza place run by an Iranian guy in the middle of Castro Valley.

Only in California.

Okay, maybe a few other places too, but none of them have a climate like this, and that's God's honest truth.

Sat down on the maroon crushed-velvet couch and leaned back. Took a good minute and a half to just breathe and remember that there weren't any gunmen after me anymore, and that none were coming. Nobody was left alive that could identify me and put me on some hit man's shit list.

Which would have been comforting, if the fact the way they'd died didn't still have me seriously off-balance. Maybe I oughta eat something after all.

Klepto seemed to agree. He rested his gargantuan cranium on my leg and looked up at me from under his peaky eyebrows, like he was thinking real hard at me: *Hey boss, what's wrong? Can't you see there's food here? It smells like they made up a whole cow just for us. Can we eat it, huh? Please? Please please please? It smells sooo good. See, I'm being a good boy and waiting. Please please notice. Why are you so bummed? There's FOOD here. Food makes everything better.*

I found a note underneath the care package.

Across the street checking on something. Back in a few minutes. Start without me. -Nya

She drew a little heart in front of her name, because that's Nya's way of making sure that you don't forget you're important.

So I started eating. The grub tasted remarkably unlike sand. Tender as a marshmallow, with great chutney and Greek salad, smoky garlic spice rub. It actually tasted so good it depressed me. Because every time I bit into it, I remembered how the one merc looked with his jaw blown off. How the other one sounded when he was trying to die in peace, and I wouldn't let him.

Fuck, Lantham, get over it.

I wouldn't, though. Not for a while. I knew that. But I still felt like a fucking chump.

Call it Catholic guilt. For all the scrapes I get into, I don't like it a bit. I like it less every time I have to kill someone.

Maybe I should take up fishing, and let Nya do the dirty work on the off chance I catch anything.

Never been fishing before. Wonder if I'd catch anything. Somewhere in the middle of wondering, I drifted off into a stare-into-nothingness. Didn't even notice I'd done it until Scuttlebutt—Nya's orange tabby—walked through and gave me a look of utter contempt, as if it were beneath my dignity to soil myself by association with Klepto.

"Oh really?" I said. "And what about the way the two of you share the couch during Jeopardy?"

She wasn't impressed. Klepto was, though—or, at least, interested. He bounded over to her and sniffed at her butt, which got him an almighty hiss, so he barked at her and smacked his front paws against the ground.

This is why cats and dogs don't get along. What one

species considers friendly, the other considers threatening, and vice versa. The best you can hope for is the kind of situation we've got here, where each party considers the other to be a mental defective, but still worth playing with.

Scuttlebutt tolerated a big lick from Klepto, then proceeded about her normal patrol duties. Klepto made to folow, but stopped when he heard me moan in pleasure around a piece of kebab.

Buzz. Buzz.

My pocket wanted me. Made me jump. I tossed Klepto a hunk of the meat and popped the phone on speaker.

"This is Lantham."

"Clarkie boy! So good to hear you've still got your voice box. No worse for wear, I fear?"

"Hi Earl. I'm fine. Whatcha got for me?"

"For you, sweetheart, I've got the world. It's sparkly."

"What about Personae?"

"Gorillas in the last rainforest, Clarke, and they found the magic beans."

"How?"

"It's like penicillin. Like gravity. Leave a gem this big laying around long enough, and someone's gonna trip over it."

"Give the the lowdown."

Earl launched into a long monologue about the technical side of things, which covered basically the same ground Jerry had, but without treating me like I didn't know anything about computers. To be fair, I'd asked to be treated like an idiot back in the forest, cause I didn't want to miss anything.

Now I was getting the high-level technical version, but it tracked pretty well with what I'd picked up already.

"Okay, I get it. What's the catch?"

"The catch? Oh, ye of little shamus. Haven't spotted the elephant yet? It ain't even painted in camo."

"Let's pretend that I got shot this morning and I'm a little slow."

"You are no fun, you know that? Gotta talk to those girls of yours, get them to scare off strawberry shortcake. You can only fuck around with feds for so long before you start wearing suits, my friend. Gotta get you back on the prowl."

"How bout you don't question my taste in redheads and I won't point out that you dress like Elton John."

"Truce declared, sweet cheeks."

"So what's the catch, he asked with unreasonable optimism."

"The catch? Oh, honey, the catch is it's a big scam."

"What kind of scam?"

"This is an open technology, Clarkie."

"Like GPL? BSD?" Different software licenses let you do different things with the tech. Some of them you can only build service businesses with, some you can build software businesses with.

"MIT."

"So, basically BSD, then. They can do pretty much what they want. Where's the scam come in?"

"Because it can't work."

"Wait...you just spent twenty minutes telling me it

could work." Now that I had some food in me, my arm was starting to throb. I got up from the couch, tramped into the bathroom, and fumbled around in the medicine cabinet. I still had some Vicodin in there from the last time I got shot.

"The *tech* works, grasshopper. The *tech*. We've all been batting this idea around since 2009. Obvious as a zit on a teenager's nose. But there's no *business* here."

"Why not...crap." I found the Vicodin, and noticed the date on it.

"What?"

"Nothing. Just realized I'm getting shot too often."

"Don't you believe it. The really satisfying injuries always hurt the most."

"Yeah, well, they don't do my brain any good. This is like thinking through LA smog." I figured expired opiates wouldn't hurt me, so I popped the lid and slammed a couple dry. "So why is there no business here?"

The front door opened. Nya came through. I mouthed Earl to her and pointed at the phone. She nodded. Then I mouthed Thank you and pointed at the food, and clasped my hands over my heart like a cartoon character falling in love.

She smiled, and hopped a bit—which, given the way her mouth extends too far and down and how square and sturdy her build is, always looks a little incongruous, if no less endearing—and skipped on through the living room. That woman may be twenty, but she's got a lightness about her that you usually only see in little kids. Something adorable—and mildly unsettling—about that.

Earl was talking out of the speaker this whole time: "The whole point of the block chain is that it's decentralized. Nobody controls it. Not a government, not a company. It doesn't work if anyone does. You can make a business running a store to trade identities and title deeds and all that good shit, but you can't make money being a trusted authority. The authority is the tech itself, and the tech is already out there."

"So what, they're pitching VCs on this thing?"

"Trying to. Got a terms sheet out in the wind. Asking for a fifty million valuation based on the strength of the patent."

"What patent?"

"They got a provisional issued last month. Exclusive blah blah blah to implement a blockchain-based mining operation for digital corporate entities, including proxies for entities, both physical and legal, so long as it's non-monetary, blah blah blah."

"That's some patent."

"It won't stand up, Clarke. Too much prior art."

"So...oh. Right." They didn't need it to stand up in court. They just had to convince someone with money that it was cheaper and easier to buy their company or pay their licensing demands than it was to litigate a patent suit. "Nice scam."

"Ain't it just? Fucking shame too. This thing's gonna turn the world on its ear sooner or later."

"Yeah, they told me. Digital title deeds, real electronic contracts signed by digital identity proxies, the whole bit."

"This scam won't do a thing for the block chain's

credibility. If these guys win, we all lose."

"How?"

"All these digital currencies—all currency if IBM gets its way—works on this tech. They get common enough, and who's left holding an empty bag? Apple and Google and PayPal all the banks and everyone else that makes money off money, they're all sitting on buggy-whip businesses. All that beautiful cash they got, all that beautiful infrastructure, all goes off to that great rust yard in the sky like yesterday's railroad tracks. Except if scams like this get too much press."

"Because then regular people won't trust it, and trust is everything in economics."

"See, I knew you had a brain."

"Okay, so this great and all, Earl, but it doesn't help me. I need to know who knows about this. Who they talked to..."

"Oh, that's *easy*, blue boy. If you'd asked me that at the outset, your bill'd be a whole lot smaller."

"Why's that?"

"Because they have a *patent*, Clarkie. The world knows."

"Fuck." So much for narrowing the field.

"Sorry to sabotage your hard-on, but reality's a cruel fucking bitch."

"Tell me about it." I rubbed my forehead. Klepto put his paws on my shoulders and tried to lick my forehead. "Okay, send the bill to Nya."

"Easier done than said. Any time you need me..."

"I'll just sing Crocodile Rock and you'll come

running."

"You're one twisted gumshoe. Don't get shot again today if you can help it." He hung up.

So, there's my day gone to hell.

IN MY LINE OF WORK, YOU'RE screwed when you run out of ideas, and I was pretty much out of ideas.

But I ignored it. I could focus on little things.

I took a swig of the Coke, bit off half of a piece of kebab, then made Klepto lay down and roll over to earn the other half. Then, a couple more bites of the rice, and I'd had about all I could stomach. It'd be better as leftovers, when I wasn't sour to other reasons. Eating something that good when you just couldn't give a damn always feels to me like you're insulting the cook.

The fridge seemed happy to see me. The little light lit up and everything.

I must've groaned or cursed, cause Nya called to me from the TV room: "Clarke? You okay?"

She didn't like hanging out in the office all day when I wasn't there, so she forwarded the phones in here and worked on her laptop when she could. Always had some nature documentary on in the background. Said she found them soothing.

This is supposed to be the part of the story where the hard-as-nails detective says he's fine, then tries to seduce the pretty girl in defiance of any plot logic. Except I wasn't fine, and Nya's my employee and my roommate, and that's just all kinds of bad juju.

And I've got a girlfriend. One I wouldn't mind marrying.

So I did the decidedly un-heroic thing. "No."

And there she was. Like magic. "What's wrong?"

Her hand was on my arm. The arm that wasn't shot to shit. I still haven't gotten used to having a family-of-sorts to come home to. But Klepto and Nya and Erica—and, until she did her runner, Rachael—made for a pretty decent family.

How do you talk to a family about the day you spent killing people in the mountains?

Well, except for Klepto, they all knew what I did. And Nya'd seen me kill people before. Only reason she was standing here breathing is I'd ventilated two people, on two different occasions, that thought she'd make a good target.

"You got twenty minutes?"

"Sure."

So I got myself some tea, on the grounds that I didn't want any more sugar, and called the dog, and went for a stroll around the back yard. I filled her in on my morning, including all the dead ends, right up to the last one where instead of a narrowing list of suspects I now had to sort through "everyone with an Internet connection."

"But Clarke," I hate it when she starts that way, because she always points out something blindingly obvious that I completely missed. "You don't need to know who knows about them. Do you?"

And, there you go. She was right. I didn't. I wasn't building a case. Even if I was, proving who was behind it would take months, maybe years, and that was time where the bad guys could make another go at my clients. I needed something more acute, and I wasn't really interested in killing anyone else today.

Or this year, if I could help it.

So, nice as putting these bozos in jail would be, the immediate problem was something else altogether. I had to stop thinking like a cop. Rachael used to lecture me about that often enough that it oughta be burned into my synapses now.

What I needed was to find a way to make the contract irrelevant. Some way my clients would get on board for.

I kissed Nya on the forehead and thanked her, then called Klepto to heel and went in to hide in my office. I stretched out on the cracked brown leather recliner—which, despite being the largest size I've ever seen, is still a little too short for me—and laid a pillow over my eyes, and started taking inventory.

Okay, Lantham, what do you have to work with. What do you know?

The clients' company, Persona, was trying to raise money for a hugely disruptive bit of tech, and they had a patent on it.

The bad guys had approached Lynn this morning at Loma Mar and blackmailed her into pressing a button at a specific location. That button triggered the bomb on the undercarriage of the car—or signled someone who did—and blew brakes on Jerry's old Jeep.

That made them crash on their way to a meet with a VC who they were pretty sure was gonna buy into their company and push them out to the public in short order.

So this was a business hit? Doing business with guns isn't exactly common around the Bay. That's more of an East Coast thing. Here, people tend to use money and computers to get the same result. So maybe whoever did this wasn't a local. If Jerry was right, there wasn't a government or a major business in the world that wouldn't kill to keep this thing under wraps.

Under wraps.

I just had to remove the business reason why killing them might make sense, then we'd be done.

Easy. I just had to convince them to release their entire business and patent catalog for free to the world. Then there'd be no percentage in killing them.

So how do you convince two middle-aged entrepreneurs who finally had a shot at the brass ring to give it all up and become free culture radicals?

This is a scam.

Did they know it was a scam they were running?

They had to. So why hadn't they just called up a patent troll and sold off the catalog?

There was something missing. Or I was seriously overestimating their intelligence.

Somewhere in the round-and-round, I fell asleep from the pain and the Vicodin. I woke up a couple hours later with Klepto licking my hand.

Wonderful thing about sleeping on a problem:

Sometimes, it solves itself.

I grabbed the office phone.

"Cal, this is Lantham. I need a favor."

5:00 PM, THURSDAY

CAL'S GOOD FOR FAVORS. One of his better qualities. So Lynn answered the phone next to her hospital bed.

"Lynn, I need to know a couple things. You're the business end of this business, right?"

"I'm the face. Palmer's our CFO."

"Right, right, you mentioned that. Palmer...Shara it was, right?"

"Yeah, that's right. What's this about?"

"Trying to figure out how to keep you all alive. Have you talked to him since this all went down?"

"Uh huh. I called when we got here, to tell him why we didn't make the meeting."

"Was he pissed?" I didn't think this guy could be behind it, but it's better to check.

"No. Relieved. Worried, too. He's here if you want to talk to him."

"I'd love to."

"Give me a second."

The phone rattled, like she'd just put it down on the counter, then she shouted. Sounded like someone came into the room, and I picked up enough of the conversation to follow that Lynn was asking someone—a woman, maybe the duty nurse?—to fetch someone else.

"Someone's going to get him." Lynn didn't even bother to pick the phone up. She just said it loud into the room. She was the kind of person that treated everyone around her according to exactly how useful they were at the moment. The world was a collection of widgets to arrange. Not exactly personable.

Usually I like that kind of casual coldness in a client. Makes life easier. Today it was just pissing me off, maybe cause I already knew it was bullshit. This woman was about as cold as a tea kettle, she just kept up the social camouflage real well. Kinda like my not-so-dearly departed brother.

But the less said about him the better.

I heard something else on the other line. A voice in the room, not the same one as before. This one was deeper.

Then Lynn said "What? How?"

The handset rattled.

"Mister Lantham?" Lynn's voice. She sounded rattled.

"Yes?"

"He's gone."

"Gone? I thought you were all in protective custody."

"We are. But he's gone. Just left. Maybe ten minutes ago."

"Do you have his cell number memorized?" She didn't have her phone with her. I still had it in my bag, since rescuing it from the car."

"Well...I think...yes."

"Good. Give it to me. Oh, I also have your laptop and your phone. Why don't you go ahead and give me passwords?"

"Why?"

"So I can look through your email and see if there's anything there that might help me track down who put the paper out on you."

"What is...paper?"

God. Fucking civilians. "The contract. Who hired the hit men."

"Oh. Uh..."

"You can change the password when I'm done. I'll bring them back to you unharmed. And if I don't act in your interest the law says that you can throw me in jail." It doesn't actually say that, but I was willing to bet she didn't know a thing about how the private snoop business works. Nobody does, not unless you're in the business yourself. It's a secret club that everyone knows about, and nobody wants to join. I mean, really, look at my day. Would you want a job like this?

"Okay, I guess that's all right."

"Good. What's the one for your phone?"

"It's a swipe pattern. Like..." She described it to me. An L for Lynn, except backwards. This, ladies and gentlemen, is why people like me and the NSA have such an easy time snooping: most people don't really think their password protects anything important, so they pick something obvious.

And she ran a startup based on a cryptographIC

protocol. Go figure.

I couldn't get too mad at her though. The Pentagon set nuclear launch codes to zero-zero-zero-zero-zero for fifty years on all their missiles just to annoy the White House. That's like installing an open window in a bank vault. The only reason any of us are alive today is that nobody tried playing a prank in a nuclear missile silo in the nineteen seventies.

"And your computer and email passwords?"

She gave 'em to me.

"Good. Now Jerry's?"

I had to wait another stretch while someone ran between rooms with a notepad. About half a cup of coffee later, she came on and read them off to me. Three of them, for one device. Dude liked his security.

"Okay, I'll track down Palmer, don't worry."

I resisted grumbling "idiot" into the phone, and I considered that an epic display of restraint.

Okay, okay, I know, customer relations isn't my strong suit.

Now, for Palmer.

"This is Palmer Shara, Personae, how can I help you?" Bored voice, younger than the other two. Sounded like he might still be in college. Didn't Lynn say she met him in business school?

"I think it's more about how I can help you, Mister Shara."

"Who is this?"

"This is Clarke Lantham..."

"You're the one who saved Lynn and Jerry today up

on the mountain..."

"That's right."

"Oh, man, I don't know what you did up there, but Lynn really hates your guts."

"I get that a lot."

"She also says you saved her ass..." he snickered like Beavis and Butthead.

"Well, someone else shot it, so it needed saving." Might as well complete the obvious joke for him.

"Thanks. We couldn't get anywhere without her. I really mean that."

I'd like to play poker with this guy. I might be able to retire. "Mister Shara..."

"Palmer."

"Fine. Palmer, I need you to focus. I'm your company's hired gun, and I might be the only thing standing between you and a hail of bullets." This is what salesmen call "escalating urgency." It definitely got his attention.

"How?"

"You've just escaped protective custody."

"Escaped? I didn't escape. I have a meeting to get to."

"With who?"

"Jimmy Calico. We missed the meeting this morning. When I found out why my partners didn't show, I sent him an email, and he's willing to meet with me solo."

"Do you have any police officers with you?"

"No. Why?"

"Well, if they tried to kill your business partners to keep them away from the meeting, they might try to kill you." Why do I have to explain these things to people?

"Oh..."

"Look, give me the location of the meeting. I'll meet you there. Meantime, watch to make sure nobody's tailing you, and if they are, don't stop at any stoplights. Whoever they are, these people aren't fucking around."

"If I'm supposed to be so worried, how do I know you're not the hit man?"

God makes people like this. I've never met any religion willing to own up to what that says about the kind of guy God is. "Ask me something that only someone who was there with Lynn and Jerry this morning might know."

"What ass cheek did Lynn get shot in?"

"The right. Came in and went out at an angle, but it came in close enough to the crack that she's probably gonna have to have stitches before she can shit normally." Might as well go for the full Junior High thing, right? That was obviously this guy's level.

"Man. Okay, you got it. I'm headed for the Fudruckers in Union Landing."

"That brings you right by my place. Where are you at right now?"

"Just crossing 24 off the Bridge."

"I'll see you there. Look for the tall guy in the green t-shirt and brown bomber jacket, driving a pink MINI."

He liked the idea, hung up.

My mouth felt tacky. All that pillow-breathing must've dried me out. I didn't feel like I'd lost any more blood, though I was hungry-tired in that kind of way you only get after you've had more blood drawn than you really ought to.

And my trusty coffee mug—the white one Nya and Rachael bought me at Dickens' Faire last year that shouted "Grouch Fuel" in letters that looked like they'd been painted with the blood of someone who woke me up too early—was trying to convince me that it had never heard of liquid, and I was an idiot for thinking it had.

"Come on, Klepto. Let's find Nya."

Just the mention of her name was enough to stir him from a nap on my chair—I don't think I'll ever get over envying that puppy's ability to nap anywhere—and into a leap at the door, which ended with a crash against the door, in one jump.

He whined and shook his head, then tried to rub it with his right paw, then looked at the door and growled as if it had intended to hurt him personally.

I reached him, scritched him below the collar. "It's okay, boy, I'll beat it up for you." And I opened the door. Beyond, the length of the main office and waiting room opened up, and it looked like Klepto was sure that whatever was out there, it ate puppies.

"Hey boy!" Nya's musical alto came from back in the file room-cum-lab. For a woman with a voice so low, she always manages to sound like some kind of spring songbird. One of a half-dozen things about her that makes her kinda spooky to be around, and lets her charm her way into anything. I play like I'm immune, because it's Nya, but the minute I forget I'm not I'm gonna wind up in deep trouble.

Klepto paused a moment, still suspicious, then, indulging in the marvelous luxury of a puppy's memory span, bounded out through the door, hung a right. A second later, I heard his tail flapping against the hardwood floor of the lab.

But Nya wasn't talking to him about how he was a good boy and a great dog. She was on the phone, talking low. Come to think of it, I couldn't remember the last time she went into the file room for any reason other to find me when I was in there dusting for prints or using the microscope.

I stepped out and peered around the double-corner. "Nya?"

She was sitting on the workbench, fumbling with her phone, trying to hang it up and looking like a guilty teenager caught toking.

"What? Oh! Hi Clarke."

I gave her a good squint. "Are you okay?"

"Fine, yeah."

Rule one in dealing with teenagers—or tweenagers—when you hear the word "fine," shut your mouth, hold onto your wallet, and grow eyes in the back of your head.

"Okay. I gotta get going, gotta keep someone else from getting shot."

"Clarke! You've..."

"I know, and once was enough. I won't get shot again, at least, not today."

She hopped down from the table, gave me a big hug. "You better not."

"I'll do what I can. Look, I left the keys for the rental on the coffee table. Could I borrow your MINI? I need something that blends in."

She snorked. "Wear your traffic-cone shirt, too."

"Thanks." I turned around and started to go, then remembered the other great bane of my existence. "Um...how're you fixed for plans this evening?"

"Three more invoices to do, then some dinner."

"You going out at all?"

She shook her head. "Not tonight."

Time was, not too long ago, she was out every night of the week. Something had changed in the last couple weeks, and she wasn't making with the explanations.

"In that case, can you run my phone down to the place on Redwood and get me a replacement with a full data transfer? Left it next to the keys."

"Yeah...uh...sure."

"What's wrong?"

She looked at me, and for just a second I thought she was going to cry. Then she blinked, and the cloud passed like a bad dream. She said "You're going back out in public like that?"

"Like what?"

She looked me up and down and giggled, which made me look down.

I saw a getup streaked with mud, mottled everywhere with splatters of blood, still damp in spots, with soot and dust on all the places that there weren't mud.

"Oh, god. I must look like I've just crawled out of *The Texas Campfire Massacre*."

"Yeah, a little bit."

"Right. I'll get changed on the way out. I'll be down at Ruddfuckers in Union City."

PALMER, I COULD SPOT FROM A MILE away if I was wearing sunglasses. He hadn't given me a description. Turned out I didn't need one. He stood out against the thrust of the neo-eclectic fascia (that's the official architectural aesthetic mucky-muck name for "early twenty-first century upscale suburban hideous") of the Union Landing shopping center like an ancient African king would stand out in a crowd of men dressed in gray flannel armor.

And yes, I'm an architecture geek. Anyone who lives in the Bay Area and isn't one is missing out on the unique joy that comes from saying "hey, what's a pre-20s Craftsman kit home doing in the middle of this row of Italianates" so often that your girlfriend refuses to go out in public with you unless it's an emergency grocery run.

But Palmer was standing in a full three-piece pinstrsipe, with tie, dark glasses, and greased-back hair in the middle of down-market suburbia—or what passes for it around the Bay—where everyone else around him, even the multi-millionaires (and, going by the numbers, there was probably at least three or four of them hanging around the shopping center this evening) were dressed in various shades of California casual. It made him look like a hit man at a pacifist rally.

He spotted me just as easy—or, at least, he stood up a bit straighter when he saw the MINI pull up. Fuddrucker's is right across a narrow parking-lot-street from the gigantic multiplex, and there wasn't any good parking on the near side, so I had to drive right past him. Heavy traffic this time of day, everyone out shopping and getting dinner. I stopped in the red zone in front of him, rolled down the passenger window, leaned across and waved.

"Palmer?"

"Yeah!" He started walking toward me.

"Stay there. I'll park and be right back."

He shrugged assent. I pulled on past the sushi place and the taquería and found a spot in the IHoP parking lot.

Swanky, right?

When I changed clothes I'd kept the getup I told him to watch for, so I wasn't exactly dressed for success myself, which means I'd have blended in pretty well if I wasn't six three and armed to the teeth. Not that anyone else could see the weapons, but unless I'm trying not to, I look like a cop had sex with a skyscraper, so I tend to have the same effect on sidewalks that Moses had on the Red Sea.

Palmer was leaning against the door jamb like a wiseguy. Where did they find this poseur? Either he wasn't a local, or he was seriously misinformed as to how things worked around the Valley.

Or he was an idiot.

I lifted my chin at him. The kind of thing you do to greet someone when you don't want to get into a loud conversation.

"Lantham, right?" he said. "The bodyguard guy. You've got your gun and everything?" At about volume ten.

Never underestimate the idiot quotient. I should have that tattooed on my left arm so I can read it every time I reach for the toilet paper.

I closed to within arm's reach. "Shut up or you'll find out the hard way. Now get inside."

"I'm supposed to wait out here."

"Tough. A man like Calico isn't going to wait out front for you if he doesn't see you out here. Now get inside." When a tall man with a gun bends over you and grits his teeth at you just right, you move. At least, if you're not an idiot.

Palmer wasn't an idiot so much as the mayor of Idiotsville. Good thing he was a coward, too. He blanched. Enough blood actually drained out of his face that he looked green. That kind of olive complexion. Maybe a kid from New York Italian who'd seen The Godfather too many times?

The kid—and from this distance I was damn sure he was barely north of twenty-three—folded like an origami swan in a sushi factory, and inside twenty seconds we were waiting in line for the golden opportunity to decide between beef, buffalo, or ostrich burgers for ten bucks a piece.

"You're not from around here, are you?" I said to him.

"What? Me?"

"You? Hell, no. I just thought talking to the flat of Dad's Root Beer might be an exciting new social experience."

"Oh." And he didn't say anything else. He wasn't even looking at the menu.

"So where are you from?"

"Who?"

"Palmer Shara."

"That's me." Looking around like a rabbit scouting for a terrier.

"What the hell is wrong with you?"

"Me? Oh..." He looked around, like he waned to make sure nobody overheard him. "Thing is...uh...well...I'm not from around here."

"Not from the East Bay?"

"Not from the West Coast."

"Really? Knock me over with a feather, why don't you?" *Right. As long as you tape it to a wrecking ball.*

"Jersey. Well...kinda." I was starting to think just about everything this kid had to say was gonna be a "kinda."

"So folks in Jersey always look around like they're expecting someone to shoot them?"

"Well, no, I mean...they tried to kill Lynn and Jerry this morning."

Captain Obvious strikes again. Still, if he was as dumb or panicked as he was playing, I wasn't going to get much out of him by leaning on him. And if he was putting on an act, I'd get better results playing up to him.

"Yeah, I noticed," I clapped a hand on his shoulder, and he jumped like my hand was an electrical lead. "Easy,

easy. Nobody's gonna try to kill you in here. Too many people. Professionals are all about not getting caught, they're not going to shoot you with all the cameras and witnesses in here. Take a breath."

He took one. Well, he more snuck one from the cookie jar so that his mom wouldn't catch him, but at least he wasn't going to fall over from hypoxia in the next sixty seconds or so.

I tried making small talk, but he didn't even look when I pointed out that he could have locally-farmed African flightless bird with a slice of avocado on top. Can't get more Californian than that without falling asleep naked on an LA beach and dying of sunstroke, right? But by the time we reached the front he was sweating and weaving all over the place, like one of those dancing windsocks outside a car dealership.

"What can I get for...sir? Are you okay?" The clerk looked to be about thirty, and had a bearing that suggested she was more than a little overqualified for the job.

"He's fine." I stepped between them so she wouldn't worry that Palmer was about to spread the Mongolian Death Flu to the other customers. "Let's see. We'll take two ostrich burgers with the works, an order of fries, an order of onion rings, and two fountain drinks."

Almost thirty-five bucks. Well, they were paying my expenses. I forked over the card, we got ourselves a table with a bead on the door so we could spot when the VC showed up.

One thing you don't get in a premium-priced

hamburger place is fast service. Middle of dinner rush like this, with people from the theater coming in, we were in for about twenty minutes of waiting.

That'd be twenty minutes too long in the company of this bozo.

I kept up with the chit-chat, and he kept looking around for an exit. Didn't matter that I told him he was safe. Didn't even matter that I showed him the revolver on my ankle and promised I'd shoot anyone who so much as looked like they wanted to punch him in the nose for being a dip shit—which, in retrospect, wasn't one of my sharper judgment calls that day. He was enough of a dip shit that he might get slugged at the condiment bar. I can just see the KTVU report now:

A local entrepreneur was killed in Union City when a fracas ensued over access to a crock of Grey Poupon. The victim was reportedly stabbed through the throat with a mustard knife by fifth grader Alice Nedall who said, quote, "That asshole was dripping sweat onto my plate, and I wasn't going to take it anymore."

It was the least stupid potential newscast my day had generated so far.

The upside to that kind of nerves: eventually you gotta talk to get it out. About halfway through the second glass of Coke—which he mixed with root beer, for reasons which completely defeated my formidable detection skills—he finally started flapping his gums.

And didn't stop.

First it was explaining how he'd just come out here from Jersey to make something of his life, like all those folks on *Shark Tank*. He wanted to be where things were happening, where he could find some way to make his fortune. He knew it was crazy expensive here, and he couldn't really afford it, but he did some couch surfing and showed up at mixers and incubators to try to hook up with some business partners.

"But crazy, you know? The crazy shit that happens. I was working out at Best Buy in Pleasanton and these two came in looking for a company phone plan. Lynn was running point, and she could negotiate like you wouldn't believe. She drove hard, got her hands on a couple of floor models of this particular sort of HTC—Jerry was really insistent, talking about rooting and sandboxing and extra cycles and everything—got 'em for cost. I've never seen that kind of savvy on the floor, and I put myself through college on sales. I know how to hustle. So I thought 'I've gotta find out what these guys do,' you know?"

"Mmm." I took a sip at him. He was sweating so much it made *me* thirsty. My encouraging noises kept him talking so I wouldn't have to worry about thinking of some way to avoid putting him out of my misery.

"So, I impressed them too. Jerry gave me a card and, whadayya know, two weeks later they're talking equity and everything. Seems like Lynn just turns everybody off, you know? Can't do the dance, can't make the romance with the money men, and they can't ever get to the table. So I got in for like ten percent and it's all wine and roses. Pretty sweet deal, lucking into something like that at Best Buy after all that work that goes nowhere, right?"

He was into the swing of the story, and wasn't looking

over his shoulder anymore. Made me a little less jumpy.

"So, this thing you guys have, this identity brokerage. Has it pissed anyone off?"

"Are you kidding? They're *drooling* over it. At least, everyone I've talked to has."

"Who've you talked to?"

"Well, Jimmy for one. Hey, where is he?"

"Don't worry, I got my eyes peeled."

"You know what he looks like?"

"Who doesn't?" I didn't really want to get into a long explanation about my history in the Valley. Painful memories, too many spider bites. I got better things to do. "Look, I gotta ask you a couple questions, and I need you to really think about it okay? Might make it easier to get a deal and see it through. I've been around the block a few times."

"Hey, hit me. I am ears." This kid really was a natural-born salesman. The further he got into the deal-talk, the more slick-cool he got. The nervous grimace started to go into a broad smile. Dude might turn into a hell of a shark one day. "You put me on the right track, maybe we can throw you a finder's fee."

"Mighty big of you."

"Who you shopping to?"

"Oh, you know, anyone we can get our hands on. It's a serious numbers game. You make a pitch, you move on. You come out with a no, it isn't a loss, cause you make a good impression, and people hear about you. They call you up. If you're doing it right."

"And you're doing it right?"

"Oh hell yeah. I mean, why do you think I got the big J on the hook here?"

The big J was right behind him, waiting in line. I had probably six minutes to wrap up my little interrogation before I had to make way for the money man.

"You haven't noticed anyone weird hanging around you recently, have you? No new girlfriends, new buddies at the golf club?"

"Oh, please. I only play golf to talk to angels."

"The track, then." Stroke his vanity, maybe it'll lead somewhere.

"Pool hall. Well, billiards. Classy places, better for meeting people."

"So, any new people? Maybe in the last couple weeks? People that were really interested in getting close to you?"

"Oh, well, you know. It ain't gentlemanly to say..."

"Tell me about her."

"We just met for pool, you know. She was there, I was there, she played with my stick and I sunk a few balls." He chuckled, like he was being clever.

"She come back to your place? You talk business?"

"Oh here? Nah. She was a burner chick, an artist. Not into the whole business thing. Anytime I'd try to talk shop she'd get bored and go find someone else to play with. Haven't closed the deal yet, but you know. Regulars are regulars, right?"

"This thing you're on. The company. What's it worth?"

"I don't know how to even start..."

"Come on, if you're shopping, you've got a valuation you're throwing around."

"Well, I was trying to negotiate a straight buyout, for like eighty mil. I figured some players around here might want it just for the troll value..."

"Protection money, in other words."

"Hey, you catch on quick," he gave me a big toothy salesman grin. "Blockchain's the next big thing, and whoever owns this patent can use it to police the field, right?"

"So what's the problem? Why not just go straight to the trolls?"

"Well, thing is, Jerry and Lynn really don't want to let it go, so I'm trying to hash out some kind of alt. If Calico wants to come as seed, well, we basically need funds to launch the main platform, so we'll need a couple hundred thou on a valuation of fifty mil. Any lower than that and I won't be able to sell it to my peeps. But if this takes off..."

"How much work to make it take off?"

"Oh, hell, no way to know. This thing makes a splash, we're gonna run into a hell of a regulatory wall, you know? We're gonna sink a load of green in just to paying the lobbyists and lawyers." His vision sounded a lot more realistic than the one I'd been pitched in the woods by his partners. "But if it works...maybe a couple billion over the next twenty years."

"A couple billion?" Or not. But, if they believed that, it might explain why they would turn down a rich buyout.

"Maybe more. It's all a lottery. It's about what the market will do. Which way it'll jump." He shrugged.

"How about Lynn and Jerry? Who inherits their stock?"

"Lynn's married, they've got a kid. So, her hubs, I guess. Jerry...I think his parents are still alive."

"He's not married? No kids?"

"Nah. If it doesn't have a screen it's not a real person to him. I think he leaves everything to his alma mater or something."

"Any of the principals well off?"

"Are you kidding? If we could get this money by mortgaging a house we would. We're all just getting by, doing this in our spare time. Well, except for Jerry. He doesn't have spare time. But he's on a military pension, so he doesn't have to worry about next month's rent."

"Wait, wait. Military pension?"

"Yeah. Navy, to pay pay for college. Went career, the full twenty. Search and rescue for a while, then went to OCS, got to be a lieutenant or something. Sub engineer, so I call him Scotty. Makes him grin. Do you know if you make someone smile, you're twenty percent more likely to close a sale? No joke. Learning that little bit is what got *me* through college. But that whole stutter thing Jer's got going on? Picked it up on the subs. Was in some kind of top secret altercation, brink of nuclear war, torpedoes, all that Tom Clancy stuff. Scared the crap out of him. He got trapped or something, and when he got out, he didn't talk for a while. When he did...well, you heard."

"Yeah, I heard." Calico was at the order counter now. "Really quick, rapid-fire. Anyone been upset that you're shopping this? Competitors? Anything like that?"

"Not that I know of."

"Anyone that really wanted to buy in they told to take a hike?"

"Nope. No offers at all yet. Today was our big shot."

"Threats? Personal grudges?"

"Nope."

"Shit."

"Wait, isn't all that a good thing?"

"Well, it doesn't tell me who might be trying to kill them." I nodded over his shoulder at the guy in the hoodie and the saggy jeans. When you're worth twenty million, you don't have anything to prove, so you don't dress up if you can help it. "Don't look now, but your money man is here."

Of course he looked. The sweat came back like magic. Maybe he wasn't worried about hit men. Maybe he was just worried about impressing the money guy.

Calico looked back. Made eye contact—with me. Not with Palmer.

And he made a beeline for the table.

"One piece of advice, Palmer?" I grumbled out the side of my mouth.

"Yeah?"

"You want a deal? Loose the tie."

Calico was definitely heading for me. I stood up. Extended a hand.

"I know you, don't I?"

"You might have seen me at a Kieretsu pitch session last year."

"Not likely. My PA's got standing orders to shoot me

if I ever go near that bunch of douchebags." And he went on for some length about what a douchebag was good for, and what exactly they could do to themselves for making startups pay to pitch. Guess I need to learn a little more about the factions in the Valley, I seem to have struck a bit of a nerve.

"I'll keep that in mind. But it's pleasure to meet you."

"And you are..."

"Clarke Lantham, Clarke Lantham Investigations."

"Wait...you were involved with Martin Galloway. You're the one who..."

"Yeah, that was me."

"Good work on that one." He finally shook my hand.

"Thanks."

"What are you doing here?"

"Who, me? Bodyguard detail. Gotta keep the talent safe. Anyway, I oughta get out of your way. Palmer, this is Jimmy. I'll be over at that table over there, give you guys some privacy."

Palmer hadn't lost the tie. I took that as a bad sign.

The restaurant was crowded, too, and I lost the race for that new seat. I wound up farther away, where I couldn't hear, but the body language told me everything I needed to know. Kid was striking out hardcore. Speaking a different language—a shame, since it was a tech area Calico was publicly interested in, at least according to the Internet. And, as we all know, the Internet knows all.

My phone rang.

I didn't recognize the number.

"This is Clarke Lantham."

"Lantham?"

At the sound of Rachael's voice, my blood went completely cold.

6:16 PM, THURSDAY

"LANTHAM, CAN YOU HEAR ME?" She sounded timid. Not a note I was used to hearing in that voice. But she had a fucking good reason to sound timid.

The sound of her voice hit the mute button on the world.

"Yeah." I didn't know whether to be happy to hear from her, or scream at her, or try to remember how to breathe. "You've got a hell of a nerve, you know that?"

"I know."

"Do you know how long..."

"I'm not an idiot, Lantham. I know."

"So what do you want?"

"I...I heard you were shot."

"Yeah, that happens when my partner isn't there to watch my back. One of those things you learn when you take your job seriously."

"Lantham...don't."

"Don't what? Don't..." I stopped. I was on the job. I couldn't afford this. "Look, I'm on a case right now. Your life isn't in danger, right? You're still breathing? Not locked up in a basement anywhere?"

"No, nothing like..."

"Then fuck you." I hung up. I could feel the steam rising off my hairline. I wanted to punch out the window, except I wasn't sitting in a booth so I didn't have easy access to a window.

Goddamn Rachael fucking Oldman. She'd better fucking die in a fire with everything she put us through.

It took me almost three breaths to think about calling her back.

Another four to start kicking myself for hanging up on her.

About sixteen hours passed before I realized that I'd shattered the hard plastic cup.

There are two kinds of adrenaline in the world. There's the good kind that floods your system when someone's shooting at you and helps you run fast enough to get away—or makes you stupid enough to run at them and beat the tar out of them while they're reloading—and then there's the bad kind.

The bad kind is like acid squirted out of your glands onto all your internal organs, and you just sort of slowly eat yourself alive.

Goddammit, Rache, I do not need this right now.

My client—or my charge, at any rate—was wrapping up his meeting, and it wasn't going well. I needed some way to calm down.

I'd have killed to have my phone back, and all my contacts. Just saying hi to Erica right now would make a hell of a difference. As it was, I couldn't even tell if she'd called me today to say hi, and I had no prayer of calling her on my own initiative, not unless I called Nya and had her look up the number, and that was a conversation I really didn't want to have right now.

Calico stood. Palmer stood. They shook hands.

The money man didn't head for the door, though. He aimed himself at me.

"Clarke, can I have a card?"

"Sure." I gave him one.

"Thanks. I might have some work for you from time to time. Due diligence stuff. You're okay with that kind of work, right?"

"Um, definitely. Sure."

We made polite hand-shaking goodbye noises, and I tried to feel good about having another potential semi-regular source of work.

But I didn't. I felt sick. I wanted to go home and walk the dog. Or take a good hard drive up Palomares Canyon.

Then, just when he was about to walk, he said, "You ought to know, these guys have made a huge stink around the Valley."

"Oh?"

"A lot of shooting from the hip at angel events. Not returning calls. Trying to dictate terms. Not a good group to do business with."

"So why did you take the meeting?"

"Sometimes, the assholes have some special magic. And if someone is trying to kill them, maybe they're on to something important."

"And...?"

"With their burn, they won't last a month. Not enough cash, not enough expertise, not willing to do what it takes to get it."

"But it sounds to me like they've got a killer app."

"A killer app doesn't make a killer business. Someone'll find another way to do the same thing, and they'll make the business end work."

"And the patent?"

He shrugged. "What you can do one way, you can do another. There's no way they'd be able to afford a serious challenge anyway."

"And around the Valley, how big a stink they made? Enough to kill over?"

"I wouldn't guess so, but you never know."

"Mind if I call you if I have some more questions?"

"Email me. Through my blog. Best way to find me."

"Thanks."

I TRAILED PALMER BACK to the hospital. He felt an obligation. I had a contract. It worked out.

Traffic was still nasty. Some kind of event tonight in the City had all of 880 North socked in like Karl the Fog. Longest, boringest road in the East Bay, and I got to spend thirty-odd miles of it looking at the ass-end of an old Ford Escort. Lucky me.

Time like that in traffic, you get a chance to think. My head was stuck in Rachael-rage, but I had to pull it out and try to do my job. I had some startup wannabes to protect. I'd been going on the notion that this was about business.

But I wasn't buying it anymore. It didn't smell right.

There are only a handful of reasons someone kills someone else, and nobody hires professional contractors in a jealous rage. You might do it to save face, but you'd have to be awfully traditional-Japanese to do that, and as far as I knew there weren't a lot of Yakuza running around the Bay these days. Not since the early nineties, and then only on the docks and in the financial district.

That left greed and insurance. If there was enough money on the line, and you could be sure you'd wind up with the fortune left over, it might be worth it.

But these guys weren't worth that. I'd just gotten that from the horse's mouth. There's a hundred reasons a guy like Calico would pass on a company—but when the reason is *they'll never amount to anything*, that takes the wind right out of my sails.

That meant there was only one reason someone would go to the trouble to call in a hit like that.

A cover-up.

They said they were coming back from meeting with Ferris out at Loma Mar.

This wasn't about the tech.

This was about Cal's investigation.

Or I was tired and pissed and jumping to conclusions. I didn't have a hell of a lot to go on. Some cases, I feel like a blind man trying to find a blank light switch in a dark room during a blackout at midnight when there's no moon out.

All of today felt like that.

"Cal, this is Lantham. You got a minute?"

"Just. We've been busy here."

"Good busy, or bad busy?"

"Someone just took another run at your clients."

"Wait, what?"

"Hospital orderly, or a woman dressed like one. Came in and tried to poison both of them. Only reason we caught it was that the husband took a drink before the patient did."

"Did you catch her?"

"Got video, but she was long gone."

"Holy shit." My boy was still in front of me, still motoring along in his Escort like nothing had happened. Cause, to him, nothing *had* happened. They hadn't gone after him. I hadn't spotted a tail on him, at Fuddruckers. Hadn't seen anyone watching him.

"Yeah, that's what I said."

"Anything to go on?"

"Not so much as a prayer."

"What about that job you..."

"I'm sorry, Lantham, but I'm being pulled away. We'll talk later. You just get home and keep your head down for a couple days, all right?"

"Right, sure." I didn't even get done with that before he hung up.

Cal wanted off that line bad. Not the kind of bad where someone had been shot. There wasn't any shouting in the background, no urgent voices, nothing like that. And it wasn't the kind where a witness was finally awake, or there was some other kind of urgent development. It had a different kind of sound. A forced, fake sound. Like he knew where I was going and he didn't want to talk about it.

So he did want off the in the worst way:

The kind of way I'd want off the line if I thought someone was listening.

Dammit, Cal, what are you dragging me into?

8:00 PM, THURSDAY

I TRAILED PALMER ALL THE way to the hospital, trailed him inside, and handed him off to the uniforms working Cal's detail. Santa Clara Sheriff's Department, every one of them. Deputies from the South Bay pulling guard duty for a hospital in the City.

Damn peculiar.

I tried to raise Cal, but he didn't have time to give me any straight answers, and strongly implied that I ought to go home before I became a resident of this luxurious iodine-scented facility.

Nya was there when I got home. She was on the phone, obviously didn't want to be interrupted. I gave her a quick hug and called Klepto to heel, set up in the TV room with Lynn's laptop and phone.

I had some digging to do. On a Mac. I hate digging on a Mac. The entire setup is designed to keep you out of the guts. I wound up spending half the night on data forensics sites looking up everything I could find on how to find information hidden on HFS+ filesystems.

The other half the night I spent reading someone else's email and texts.

Something about Lynn had made her a good leverage target. Was it just because she had a family? Or was there something else about her, something that made her uniquely vulnerable? Maybe the same thing that made her a target for the hit men rather than just a target for leverage.

They'd gotten her to trigger that bomb herself...

Unless, of course, that had all been a ruse, and she'd arranged the whole. Had she known enough to hide behind the engine block when the bullets started flying?

I thought back. I was sure I remembered having to forcibly relocate her to keep her out of the "Best Swiss Cheese" competition. Not that that proved anything. People did stupid things when they dipped their toes into violence. They thought watching movies gave them an idea of how things worked.

So what if Lynn had called in the hit? What did she have to gain? Nothing in those emails that suggested she wanted anything more than to build a company and change the world—modest ambition for this neck of the woods—or that Jerry stood in her way. They seemed to be in lockstep all the way down the line, and their correspondence went back a good twenty years. Old friends, always looking for a way to change the world together.

If it was something personal, there were cheaper ways to do it. Lynn wasn't exactly rolling in it. Oh, she wasn't hurting quite as bad as Palmer thought she was, but I took a look through her browser history and found all her bank accounts. Or, at least, the standard spread you'd expect of a middle-aged professional. She had a decent retirement built up, hadn't made any draws on it. She rented her house. She had a kid just starting college that would drain most of her savings, something she fretted about in her correspondence. She seemed to be on good terms with her husband—her communications with him were cordial if not exactly steamy, and she didn't say anything in any of her other communications that would lead me to believe it was anything other than a comfortable, decent marriage.

She even went to church. Granted, I'd been down in the weirdness that passes for good behavior in churches in the last year, but Lynn was more like what I expected from my Catholic upbringing. Once or twice a week in church, religiously (if you'll pardon the pun—I get kinda punchy late at night). A social ritual.

Not a swanky Danville or San Francisco church either, but a little local charismatic place in West Oakland. Seemed to believe it—she quoted scripture in her personal correspondence and had a line from the twenty-third Psalm on the Kincaid painting on her desktop, but it seemed like an all-American kind of religion, the kind that has a strong separation between church and bank. Jesus was lord of her heart—money was lord of her business.

SOMEWHERE AROUND THREE IN THE morning, Nya came in, all bleary eyes and yoga pants and hips.

"Heya."

She rubbed her eye and gave me a smoky "Hey. Can you turn the movie down?"

"Oh. Sorry." I had a queue of 80s action films on the

big screen, for background noise. I turned down *Die Hard*. What can I say? Day like today, explosions and gunfire help me relax. Call it a sickness. Doc Samson sure does.

"Thanks." She tottered over to me and flomped down on the long low chesterfield next to me. She then timbered over onto me, leaning as I was against the right arm rest. "Why you working so late?"

"Trying to figure out who called in the hit team. I can't even figure out why anyone would want to kill these people."

"Ordinary?"

"Aside from having the kinds of social skills that would horrify a high school principle, yeah."

"You got through everything yet?" She took my coffee cup from the pine tray table, then took a sip.

"Hey hey, coffee theft is not part of the roommate deal."

"Roommate shmoommate, we're family and you know it."

"Yeah, well, don't go crowing too loudly about that. When I get killed they'll think you did it for the insurance." I took my coffee from her and protected two big swallows of it from further annexation.

She bapped me on the arm. Right in the shredded muscle.

"Ow!" I yelped, woke the dog. Then I winced, hiss-breathed through my teeth. Tried like hell not to start screaming at the top of my lungs. "God...dammit, there's a bullet wound there."

"Oh, god, Clarke, I'm sorry..." She reached for me, then jerked her hand back like she'd touched a hot stove, then did it a few more times. Looked like she was trying to speed-sculpt a massive spider out of thin air, and was really worried about getting it just exactly right.

"It's fine," I hissed, "I have a whole other arm. I can get by without that one. Why the ever-loving fuck did you do that?"

"I forgot."

"Gah. Serves me right for wearing a pullover. You might get that insurance sooner than I thought."

"Clarke, stop." She always uses my name like that. Like you always use a child's name in order to get its attention. It's one of those things she does that tells you your family. She has a hundred little ticks like that, and every one of them drives me nuts. "You're not gonna get killed."

"Just keep telling yourself that."

"Clarke," her voice gets plaintive when she's serious. It's a sound that reaches down into your brain and sets massive grappling hooks on the inside, "Stop it. You have to stop. Don't joke about that, okay? Not ever."

"What..."

"I mean it. Stop."

Something down in my bones sat up on its hind legs and stuck out its claws. "Care to explain why?"

"Only if you tell me why you hung up on Rachael today."

"That was her you were on the phone with in the file room." It wasn't *quite* a growl.

"Yeah."

"How long've you been talking to her?" *Shut up, Lantham, stop it before you break something else.* Trouble was, after this morning, after the last six months, I just wanted to strike a match and set the whole damn world on fire. "What's her damage, anyway? What the fuck. And...wait, hold on, have you been talking to her all this time? Do you know where she is?" I wasn't sure I wanted the answers to those questions. Didn't want to find out I couldn't really trust her.

"No. Just since last week. She won't tell me where she is."

"No luck tracing her phone?"

"Clarke, she doesn't want to be found. Give it up."

"Oh, come on. If you haven't tried to run a trace you're not half the mama bear I take you for."

"I promised I wouldn't..."

"Fine. Get the hell out of here."

"Clarke!"

"I mean it. I've had enough of the wringer she's put me through, and if you're gonna play her games, you can fuck off too."

This is how people lose their families, talking to them like this. I knew it even as I said it, but I didn't care. I'd had a bellyfull of life in general and didn't much care who knew it.

She squirmed, turned away. Looked at the open French doors that separate the TV room from the landing. I heard her breathing change. She was crying, and didn't want me to see it. Probably didn't want me to accuse her of being manipulative, which I probably would have. But I could see she was making an effort, and all six feet three of me felt like it wanted to fold up and hide in a matchbox.

She spoke to the other room, in that voice that, more than a year and a half ago now, convinced me to put my life on the line to save her from her father and her boyfriend that night they tried to kill her. "Tell me about her. Your client."

Who'da guessed that voice would mean I'd wind up saddled with her for life? Or that I wouldn't resent it, at least not too much. At least, not when I wasn't being an asshole.

"Eh, not much to tell." I skipped the apology, since she obviously didn't want it. Showing her she was still welcome, that was more important. Besides, she had a way of looking at things that sometimes shook weird corners out of cases. "She's just an ordinary..."

Klepto went from sleeping to fully awake and running down the stairs, started scratching at the back door.

"Oh hell. Just a sec." I lifted the tray table containing Lynn's computer and swung it wide, then stood up enough to shift the one containing mine. I was still dressed. Still had my shoes on, because I was too antsy to kick them off. Post-gunfight jitters can do that to me. I was still rattly from my morning in the mountains twenty hours ago, and didn't want to relax too much in case I needed to get somewhere in a hell of a hurry.

I let Klepto out the door at the bottom of the stairs, then followed him. The early-morning was deep enough that I didn't want to just leave the door open for him. A house this old already leaves a bit to be desired in the insulation department, I didn't see any reason to turn it into a fridge as well.

On the other hand, I could probably use a walk. Walks are good for cooling off. Night air does something to the gravelly heart of a grouchy gumshoe. I grabbed his leash off the hook by the back door and coiled it in my hands just in case I decided to take him with me.

I rounded the corner of the house—right out the back door, then another right about five feet later when the side-path opened up into the field-like back yard—and decided I was gonna need to take him on that walk. Poor guy was stir crazy from me having been gone and/or sleeping all day.

Except, he wasn't stir crazy. I could see him in the light of the motion detector floods. He was sniffing all around like mad, but wasn't fertilizing anything.

Something had him in a lather.

Then, out in the middle of the yard—a good ten yards away—he started whining and running in circles.

"Klepto! Klepto, what's wrong?" I jogged out into the sea of unkempt and half-dead grass—guess I haven't seen a lot of sense in keeping up with the landscaping since Rachael skipped town. "Klepto, are you...whatcha got there, boy?"

He was nibbling on something.

Actually, he was full-throated gnawing on it.

I reached him, knelt down.

He had a butcher-fresh bone in his mouth. Looked like a lamb's leg.

I hadn't given him a bone in days. And Nya hadn't been to the grocery store.

My stomach did a quick flip, then decided that wasn't enough and did a couple more. I grabbed for the bone.

He snarled at me. Cute from a puppy, dangerous from a teenage mutt that's half your size and protecting a prize. I didn't even stop long enough to think. When he dropped the bone to snarl I whipped it out from beneath him. When he lunged in to bite me and take it back, I slapped him.

Klepto whined. I didn't blame him a bit. I'd have whined, or worse, in his place. The theft and the betrayal in a one-two punch can't have made much sense to a puppy. But I had to get it away from him before he ate enough of whatever poison was smeared on the thing.

And it was smeared on it. It was making my hand tingle.

"Come on, boy. Inside."

He looked at me, suspicious, but when I started moving he fell to heel automatically.

I blundered up to the door, trying to stay calm enough to think well enough to save him. I needed to call the animal equivalent of poison control, whatever that was, and find a twenty-four hour vet, and...

As my hand touched the doorknob, I saw a figure out of the corner of my eye. Hiding in the bushes up beside the front of the house, right where you could cover both entrances.

I didn't stop. I went the rest of the way inside.

Closed the door, locked it behind me quietly, then

bounded up the stairs two at a time.

Nya was still in the TV room.

"Nya, Klepto's been poisoned. No, don't say anything. I need you to get him to your room, and figure out how to call poison control. I don't know what they did it with, but it's on this," I held out the bone, "I'm gonna put it on the table. Get in your room and stay there until you figure out what to do with him. We've got a prowler outside, I've gotta catch him before he gets away."

Her face went from horrified to determined, as if she had just downshifted her internal transmission. She stood up, smiled at Klepto, and led him to the front of the house.

People that are good in a pinch are the hardest people in the world to come by. I was going to have to eat a lot of crow for snapping at her—she wouldn't make me, but if I didn't I'd carry the guilt around for months. Like she said, we're family, blood relation or not, and she's more than earned the benefit of the doubt from me.

I followed. Killed the lights as I went, everything except the TV room. I needed to be able to spy out without being spotted.

There are two ways to do security. Option one: Close everything off so nobody gets in. Option two: open everything up so you can see them coming. The only prayer you have in this house was if you picked option 2. The living room is right at the front of the house, occupies the entire northwest corner of what's essentially a big cube—it's one of those old pre-war hand builds that was   designed   by   someone   without   a   lot   of imagination—and the front door leads out onto a big porch at the front. It's got windows all around, big enough for me to duck through, and I'm not exactly a hobbit.

I hooked a left in the living room, a right at the hallway, turned on my bedroom light, closed the door.

The guy I'd spotted—at least, I assumed it was a guy because nine times out of ten, violent felons are—had been crouching behind the camellia bush right at northwest corner of the house. From that position, you can see the front and back door, and the only other ways out of the house are through windows, which is why he set up there. I needed to know if he was still there.

I squatted low and slunk up to the windows right at the edge. Stayed low, didn't open the blinds. There wasn't anything backlighting me, no way for him to see I was there as long as I didn't do something stupid, like slipping and jostling the blinds.

Behind me, and around the corner, I could hear the barest throbs of Nya's voice bleeding through the walls. Controlled, almost calm, because it was life-and-death for a family member, but the terror was there. Seeping in through my pores. Like I didn't have enough of my own.

I put my eye up to the thread-hole in the blinds. Took me a few seconds to focus and adjust to the dark.

Then he moved. Slipping out of the bush. Moving toward the back of the house. Maybe going to recon things from the rear. Was he trying to break in? Was he going for the office in the detached garage? Or maybe the MINI. If he was wanting to rub me out, that would be a hell of a way to do it. And these bastards seemed to have a thing for car bombs.

But why now? Why here? It wasn't like anyone could have followed me from the gun fight this morning. All three of those guys were dead, and one of them was burned to a crisp, and good riddance.

So how had they found me? Were they tailing Palmer? Did they pick me up at Fuddruckers? Why wait till three in the morning to fuck with me?

He's definitely heading round the back.

That's the break I needed.

I still had Klepto's leash in my hand when I slipped out the front door and closed it whisper-soft behind me. Down the concrete stairs, right at the bottom, and following the poured-concrete sidewalk that circled the house like a suburban athletic track.

I peered around the corner, looked back along the edge of the house.

It was a man. Smaller than me, which took him firmly out of the "freak of nature" category. About five ten, sturdy build, moved like the top salesman on a car lot.

The back door had a big window in it—thick plexiglass so it wouldn't be easy to break into—and he was leaning up right to it to see what he could see looking through any peek holes in the way the curtain fell.

He'd left the gate open. I could get right up behind him, if I got through when he looked the other way. If he was looking for an entry, he'd want to make sure the room was clear, and get in and get control of it.

The whole house is a little under forty feet long. Not a

lot of ground to cover at a quick stride, and not too much more if you're rigging it for silent running.

But he didn't look the other way. He squatted down and produced a couple lock picks from his pocket and started jiggling the lock.

I waited for him to spring the thing, then, as he was stepping in, I sprang round that corner. Kept quiet, light footed as a guy like me can get, and let my sneakers earn their name. Covered the distance in for loping strides. He was just inside on the landing, hadn't made a move up the stairs yet.

I came right up behind him with the metal clip on the end of Klepto's leash, and pressed it into his back.

"Don't move, buddy, or I redecorate my stairwell. This is a .44 magnum, big enough to blast your kidneys all over the carpet and keep going."

He tensed, like he was going to try to fight back. I lifted my right leg and stomped down on the back of his knee.

He oofed, went down onto the up-stairs. His kneecaps clacked against the thin carpet, and I forced him down flat and twisted his back hand up behind him.

"Nya! Nya!" Much as sound leaked in this house, it was big enough and twisty enough that you really had to bellow to be heard in the bedrooms from the stairwell.

She started moving. I passed the time it took her to make it to this end of the house by saying things like "Like poisoning puppies, you son of a bitch? How'd you like to find out what drain cleaner does when you squirt it up someone's nose? I know a lot of nasty tricks they don't even prepare you for in spec ops training."

I wouldn't actually do that to someone, not really, but you gotta admit it's creepy as hell, and that's kind of the point. When you gotta get information out of someone, there's only a few ways to do it: you can scare them, you can hurt them, you can engage their self-interest, or you can get them to like you. Making them like you works best, but that takes a lot of time, the kind of time I didn't have. Hurting them doesn't work, because they'll say anything to make it stop. It also gives you nightmares, the kind that don't go away for a long time.

A very long time.

Scaring them, though, that works wonders. Not as reliable as when they like you, but it'll do in a pinch. And it's worked for me before.

This guy squirmed, but I had him locked in tight. He was strong, though, and I was tired. If I had to hold him like this for too long I might wind up on the losing end of the stick.

Nya and Klepto got to the top of the stairs. Nya took one look at my entanglement and said "Woah."

"Duct tape?" I said.

"Sure." She disappeared, leaving a bewildered and not-entirely-well looking Klepto at the top of the stairs to figure out what was going on.

I could hear Nya rifling around in the kitchen and shouted "Grab the twelve-gauge, too. This guy's got some fight in him. We might need the insurance."

"The big one or the small one?"

"Get the small one. It's got buckshot. Leaves big

raggedy holes. What did poison control say?"

"ASPCA. They have to know what he ate." She appeared again at the top of the stairs, a roll of duct tape in one hand, the shotgun in the other, pointed up.

"Excellent." I reached for the tape. "Chamber a round, get a good bead on this guy's head."

She racked the slide and pulled the butt to her shoulder. The thing was just-barely legal at eighteen-and-one-thirty-second inches, and loaded with full-charge double-ought hunting rounds.

Duct tape makes a sound like a robot crash-landing in a boulder field when you rip it open, and it tastes like rubbing alcohol and used tires, but you can't beat it for improvised handcuffs. I lashed the prowler's chicken-wing tight on the skin, then, with my knee holding it in one place, bought his other arm up and lashed it to him. He wiggled, tried to trick me into letting some slack in, but I've done this too many times to fall for that.

I've also had too many arguments with Rachael about proper rope technique, which she used to keep getting me into despite my solid wish to keep the relationship purely professional. I think she did it just to annoy me—irritating Lanthams seems to be an Oldman family hobby.

"Now, we can talk." I yanked him up by the duct tape, careful to be as un-gentle as possible. He was none-too-steady on his feet—the knee I kicked didn't seem to be holding his weight right, and he grunted every time he moved.

I plopped him down on a chair in the kitchen, taped his feet to the legs, taped his arms to the chair back.

Didn't quite mummify him, but I didn't worry too much about the cost of duct tape.

"First things first. What did you give my dog?"

Dude said squat. Just looked at me with that look in his eyes like he could take whatever I dished out, cause he'd seen worse than me.

I was close to blind panic, and I figured, after this morning, what's one more corpse in my life. I wound up to lay into him with the kind of haymaker that would feed a whole herd of horses...

...when Nya put her hand on my cocked forearm.

"Clarke, let me."

"You?"

"Me. Take Klepto out back, let me talk to him."

I wasn't happy about it, but if I stayed I might kill him before I got enough out of him to save Klepto, so I left her there. Nya has ways, and I've learned, the hard way, to trust her instincts. She's not always right, nobody ever is, but she's saved my life almost as many times as I've saved hers, and that's a hell of a record.

So I went outside to get some air.

Klepto followed me.

But he wasn't walking straight.

3:52 AM, FRIDAY

THE MOTION DETECTOR LIGHTS SNAPPED on as soon as I set foot beyond the edge of the house into the back yard proper. The large concrete patio pad blasted the light back at me.

Klepto walked ahead. He stopped a couple times to double back, as if he was trying to figure something out, then he'd shake his head and lope forward.

I followed him. One foot in front of the other. He'd been a birthday present, six months ago. Now that stupid little hellhound was about to break my heart.

Stupid? No. Not stupid at all. I know everyone with a dog says this, but Klepto was a brilliant little sonofabitch. I'd been thinking about getting him trained to track people. I've still got some friends on the force in the K9 unit. If I had more time, maybe...

You're wasting it, Lantham. You've got a few minutes before Nya calls you back in. You've got nothing else to do. Take the time you've got.

Sometime the voices in my head are a lot smarter than I am.

So is Klepto.

He padded his way to me with something in his mouth. He laid down on the ground at my feet and dropped a ball. It lay dead in front of him. He looked up at me and whined at me.

"Okay, boy. Okay. I'll play." I smiled. Tried to seem chipper. Tried to keep my eyes clear so he wouldn't freak out.

I picked up the ball, tossed it. Klepto lurched to his feet, bounded after it, captured it, and brought it back to base. I tossed it again.

He returned for another round, and another but he was moving slower. Like a car running out of gas, grinding to a stop.

So I sat on the ground, and pulled him into my lap, and patted his flanks. Petted his head. Let him lick my face. He was already too big for this, but what the hell. It wasn't like I'd have another chance to get my hips strained by his weight.

Sitting there, I looked around for something else to watch. I couldn't bear to look at him. Just wanted to feel him breathing, for as long as it would last. His breathing, at least, was still strong, even if the rest of him was going loose and floppy. The rest of the patio wasn't very interesting. The rest of the back yard, well, I'd seen it a million times, except...

What is that?

Something crawling near the door to the offices. Looked for all the world like an industrial-sized rat. Maybe the size of a football.

Possum? I'd seen them around here before. Not

anything worth getting worked up over. At that point, I figured I was pretty well out of "up" to work.

Then, the possum disappeared through the closed office door.

"What the hell?" I slid Klepto off my lap, jogged to the office door.

It was standing open.

Light switch. Now I could see. Nobody in there. Not like it's a difficult space to clear. Three rooms, only one interior door, the one to my office. I peered around Nya's desk enough to be satisfied that nobody was hiding in the file room. Her drawers were all open, bits and bobs had fallen onto the floor. Someone had been in here and gone through everything. The file room was torn apart too—not exactly raped-and-pillaged, but definitely assaulted and harassed for no apparent reason.

I kicked my office door in. It swung all the way around and banged the wall.

My office was in half-shambles too. That prick had already been in here and done a sneak around the whole place. This wasn't the classic burglary shtick where you poison the dog to make off with the guns and jewels in the house. This was an information hunt, and I only had one case going that even might revolve around trade secrets or anything of the sort.

This bastard poisoned my dog to get the info I was holding. He couldn't know I had the laptops and the phone, so maybe he was convinced I'd written something down or...

Or he'd followed me from the hospital. Where he'd

been hanging out all day. Maybe posing as an orderly in drag. And overheard Lynn giving me the passwords to her phone and computer and Jerry's computer.

It was the only thing that fit.

And if this wasn't personal, if it really was about business or a cover-up or something, then it probably wouldn't matter if Jerry and Lynn survived another few days...

...as long as whatever evidence they were after didn't.

I burst out of the garage, locking the door behind me out of habit. I sprinted across the yard, slowing down just enough to scoop Klepto's now-comatose body up into my arms, and kept on sprinting into the house, up the stairs, and around the corner into the kitchen.

Nya wasn't there.

The prowler was there, looking slightly bewildered.

"Where is she?" Something in my voice, or maybe the fact that I was holding the dog he'd tried to kill and looking at him like I wanted to remove his spleen with a cocktail fork, put a shock of terror into him that threatening him with a gun hadn't. His eyes went wide-white, and he weakly jerked his head toward the living room.

"In...in there." He gulped hard.

I crossed the kitchen, didn't find her in the living room, but heard her muffled voice from the bathroom to my left.

"Nya?"

She opened the door, gave me a little nod of acknowledgment and plugged her other ear so she could concentrate on the phone. Then she said: "Yes. Yes, I understand. Thank you so much. You have no idea. Really."

She hung up. She ran to me and hugged me and gave me a big kiss on the cheek.

"What's that for?"

"He's going to be okay?"

"How do you know?"

"He told me." She pointed at the guy in the duct tape. Evidently he couldn't bring himself to kill a dog. People were okay, but not dogs. So he smeared the bone with some lidocaine and morphine, enough to make the mutt happy and put him to sleep, but not enough to kill him—or, at least, that's what he thought.

But we needed to be sure, because the treatment for an overdose could kill him if he hadn't actually overdosed.

I went to the sink and reached underneath. I had Nya turn him so he could see me. "So how much, exactly, did you give him?" I pulled out a bottle of Drain-o and set it on the table, then went to a generic baking stuff drawer.

"I don't know, man, I don't know, I'm not a vet or anything, you know..." His eyes, wide and trying really hard not to look like he wanted to crawl under the chair and squeal in terror, fixed on the Drain-o bottle. Guess he remembered the sweet nothings I'd whispered in his ear.

"Oh, come on, you have to know. You bought it, right?" I pulled a turkey baster from the drawer and set it next to the bottle. "You smeared it all over the bone. Look, I'll make you a deal, I'll tell you what I know, and you tell me what you know. And, if we're lucky, we can trade without having to get nasty. Fair, straight-up horse trade."

I waited for him to reply, then cut him off just as he pulled his breath in. "You see, we've got a couple things in common, and that's how you build relationships, right?"

Twist the top off the drain cleaner.

"We're both hired guns. You've been hired to get rid of my clients, and I've been hired to keep them around."

Peel back the safety seal.

"Now, I know that sounds like we're on opposite sides, but here's the thing," I stuck the turkey baster into the neck of the bottle, "We're not actually involved, you and me. We're just doing a job. We don't have a vested interest. We're just...playing on opposite teams."

I drew a full measure of the thick clear caustic up into the turkey baster, and removed it from the bottle.

"And normally, I'm okay with that. But from where I'm sitting, you broke the rules."

I carefully, and unhurriedly, replaced the serrated yellow cap.

"It's one thing to go after my clients. That's your job, and I respect that. My job would be to stop you, and you respect that. So far, so good."

I replaced the bottle under the sink, then retrieved the baster. I held it, bulb down, business end up, in front of me, and advanced on him.

"And you came here looking for something, I can respect that too. I might have done the same thing if I was in your position."

I was standing in front of him now. He was looking up at me, eyes complete glass, his whole body covered in sweat. I could feel his breathing, through his nose, against the front of my shirt. It was taking everything he had to hold it together.

"But when you attack my family, that's different. And the great thing is, I have a big basement here. A *big* basement. The kind of place a body can go undetected for *years*. The kind of place you can wait for all the decomposition to happen, then start feeding the bones out in the trash one at a time, and nobody ever finds it out. And these walls? They're old-style lath and plaster. Nice thick things, good heavy oak framing. And all the trees around them? It's as close to soundproof as you can get."

I moved the turkey baster to under his nose.

"I don't have any problem playing dirty if you don't. How's this smell? Burn?" I didn't have to ask. He was grunting and shaking his head, trying to keep it from wafting up and burning out his sense of smell. "So all you've got to figure out is: how in are you? Is your client really worth this? Or do you think maybe we can make a deal? Because if my dog dies, buddy...well, I love that dog. I love him a lot more than your mother loved you. You know what I mean?"

He nodded. A stiff, forced nod.

I didn't move the turkey baster. I did get a hank of his hair in my hand and hold his head absolutely still.

"How much morphine did you smear on that bone?"

"About..." he swallowed, "About...um...I don't know. A

test tube worth, I guess."

I looked at Nya. She nodded. Started dialing again.

"What were you looking for out there?"

"The laptop. They wanted the laptop."

"Who are *they*?"

"How should I know, man?"

"Then who are you?"

He tried not to answer. So I held his hair so tight it nearly ripped his hair off, and I pressed the turkey baster to his upper lip.

"Who are you?"

"Sanchez. Jaime." With the 'h' sound for the 'j'.

"Where you from, Jaime? Who hired you?"

"Miami. I...I...Stillwater. I work for Stillwater."

Oh, fuck me. I let him go, pulled the baster away. "Well, not anymore." I squirted the baster into the sink, tossed the empty in after the liquid. "Nya?"

I poked my head into the living room. She had one of the table lamps on, and she was injecting something into Klepto.

"What is it?"

"Naloxone." From her overdose kit. Nya had a heroine problem a while back—her dad got her hooked on it, for reasons that still turn my stomach. I got a kit to keep around in case she ever falls off the wagon. "They said to give him a little, just to be sure he didn't stop breathing. He should come out of it in a few hours. Clarke..." She looked up at me, and caught my eye, and I think for the first time since I met her I saw the real her.

The part of her that could survive anything, that took care of anyone she considered family. Something inside her that was fifty years old, even though she was barely twenty-one. "Find out what's going on, please."

I nodded. "I promise."

That's a kind of sacred trust we've got. It was never official, it just happened. I don't break promises to Nya. She doesn't break them to me. That's the deal.

I turned around, strode back through the kitchen to the landing at the top of the stairs, hung a right into the TV room and grabbed my temp phone. Nya had gotten the replacement like I asked, but I hadn't activated it yet, so I was still using the pre-paid.

"Hello, Sheriff's Department? I've captured a prowler. Can you send somebody by?"

POLICE SERVICE IS ONE OF THOSE industries that people in the Valley would say is "ripe for disruption." Slow, clumsy, ham-fisted, and does that same thing to the people its supposed to serve that cable companies and proctologists do to their customers, and without anesthesia.

It took them twenty minutes to show up, and a further forty minutes to finish taking my statement and decide that I probably was the injured party and they shouldn't arrest me just for good measure. Evidently the dogma since I was drummed off the force had changed, and nowadays being the victim of a crime is grounds for police suspicion.

Especially in the opinion of one Deputy Simpson, who seemed to think that the fact that I subdued the prowler and tied him up not only made me guilty of assault, it also proved I was too dangerous to be let out on the street alone at night. I wound up having to pull the professional courtesy card, show her my retirement shield, and talk about being a brother cop in order to avoid waking up my lawyer.

If I'd just killed the bastard, they'd have let me alone. In a home invasion you're presumed to be within your rights to defend yourself. But if you don't kill the trespasser, that somehow proves you weren't afraid for your life, and so any actions you take must have been malicious.

Thank God I've got a good lawyer.

I wound up getting rid of everyone before the sun had peeked over the hills out the back windows. Klepto was still asleep, but he was breathing. Nya was curled up with him on the living room couch, so I left them be, went back to the TV room and kept working on my all-nighter.

They wanted the laptop.

But I hadn't found anything interesting on Lynn's laptop. I'd looked, and looked deep. I'd done data forensics tricks to find stuff she might have deleted, to look for hidden partitions, I'd even opened the thing up to look for spare memory devices that had to be plugged in physically, but no dice.

I hadn't, however, gotten to Jerry's laptop yet.

Taking Lynn's apart was child's play. Jerry was a paranoid data geek, and it showed. It took me the better part of two hours for my sleepy brain to tumble to the way he'd organized his byzantine directory structure.

His browser history turned up a couple interesting wrinkles. Dark Reading contributor's credentials, for one. That told me a lot about the kind of guy I was dealing with, which gave me some ideas about what to look for. Someone this deep in hackerville, especially someone working on cryptocurrencies and related tech, would probably be using mail drops and other anonymous services on the Dark Web—and probably also using an onion router to play around on top-level domains.

I needed a hidden TOR installation. There wasn't one on his normal login, and I couldn't find any other user accounts. If he was using a boot stick, I was sunk—those things don't keep any history to comb through, and they even mask the MAC address of your device. Perfect anonymity unless you hit a honeypot or another identity trap someone's set up for you on the Dark Web.

But if I was spending a lot of time in the dark, unless I was really intentionally doing criminal things, I'd just want privacy and a little anonymity. I might just make a bootable hidden partition. Think of it like a secret room in a house, with a door to the outside disguised to look exactly like the exterior wall. I'd put it on my main drive or one of the extras I always kept with me.

I poked around, found the partition editor. It didn't look like there was anything on the resident drive.

I hate dead-ends.

But in the laptop's carry case, I found a thin little solid-state drive. I plugged it into the laptop, rebooted the thing, popped into the BIOS and directed the computer to boot to the external.

I got a boot loader. A small partition, dumped me right to an xmonad session (one of the more obscure and difficult to navigate Linux desktop managers—if you don't know, you really don't need to, and it'd take too long to explain anyway). I had to fumble a bit to figure out his key bindings, but after about ten minutes I managed to open the extra special hacker version of Firefox and comped through it for passwords and history.

And I got really lucky.

He was a member of several double-blind dead drops for the press. Media leak sites created after the Snowden incident made it even more difficult for whistleblowers to get information to the media without getting arrested. Never underestimate the lengths people will go to for National Security—trust me, I date a Fed, and some of the stuff she yawns at would curdle your toenails. She might not exactly share top secret info across the pillow-tops, but you can tell a lot about what a person thinks is normal by how they react when you're talking shop.

Sometimes I wonder how she can sleep at night, and then I remember how she puts me to sleep, and I get more annoyed that she has to take these long-ass assignments.

Jerry's computer told me he was into some serious anti-establishment stuff. His current crusade was the officer-involved shootings in the Valley, the kind of crap that had wrecked my morning commute. I don't listen to the news much anymore, so I didn't know what anyone was reporting, but I didn't expect this.

It wasn't just Santa Clara county. It was San Mateo, too. And San Francisco. He'd been looking at them all, and collecting, stories, and he'd been logging into media dead drops.

A lot of them.

Every local paper that ran one, actually. Some of the national ones, too.

What had he been dropping? What did he have other than rumors and curiosity?

Would it be on the computer? Would he keep it with him?

Come on, Lantham, what would he be dropping to all those outlets...

My brain was too sleepy to unlock it, and I couldn't very well go through and look at every image, sound, video, text file, and animation on a computer with a packed-full 6TB hard drive on board and another 3TB drive outboard.

I stared at the computer for a long time. Long enough that morning peeked over the mountains and slapped me in the face.

I decided to give up and head to bed for a while. Maybe a nap would turn up something useful.

A grand idea. It almost lasted long enough to get me off the couch to lock up.

I FOUND OUT THE HARD WAY that I'd fallen asleep working when Nya decided to inflict breakfast on the house.

At least there was bacon.

But it wasn't the bacon that woke me. Or the hideous-smelling pancakes.

It was the disturbingly wet tongue backed up by breath straight out of the pit of hell.

"Klepto?"

Yeah, yeah. I'm here. Weird night, huh? Weird dreams, too! Are you gonna feed me now? And pet me? Oooh, petting would be sooo good. I'll keep licking you if you pet me, promise. I'l never never never stop cause...oooh, yeah, right there. Right between the ears.

And then he figured he'd kick the floor for a while. I don't know if that's a standard feature with this particular variety of mutt, or if the drugs last night cross-wired his brain and he got a firmware upgrade, and frankly, I didn't care.

I also wasn't expecting my eyes to leak like that, but Klepto seemed to like the salt, so I figured it was okay.

"Damn, boy, I knew I liked you, but I had no idea." Not that it's my fault. We co-evolved with dogs, so we're programmed to like them more than people.

At least, that's my excuse.

I pulled myself up to something approaching vertical and lumbered, all limbs and bleary eyes, into the land of dubious calories.

At least there was bacon.

And, with enough bacon, there was enough Lantham to catch up with what I'd read this morning.

"Nya? You've been listening to the news this week, right?"

"When I'm in the office, yeah. Why?"

"Anything interesting?" I could have gone to look it up online—would have last night if I'd been anywhere close to awake, but I had a lap full of pancake-hungry, happily not-dead monster puppy cranium and a plate full of bacon and oranges, and I wasn't about to get back to work until I was good and fed.

"Interesting ha-ha, or interesting dangerous?"

"Anything."

"I don't know. People dying. Stock market going up and down. Cell phone pictures." She shrugged. "Want another pancake?"

"Ah, no. I'm fine."

"Rachael was right about something, you know," she said.

"What?"

"You can't lie for anything."

"Thanks, I love you too." The mention of Rachael drained everything left of my appetite. I got up, made to leave. Stopped at the door. "Thanks for breakfast. And...I'm sorry I was a dip shit last night."

She didn't tell me it was okay. Not this time. I couldn't blame her. It wasn't okay.

But she did nod at me. And smiled a little bit, too.

You're gonna be weeks paying off that slip of temper, idiot. Stop looking for absolution and get the job done so she and Klepto are safe.

"Thanks for the phone."

"You're welcome."

"SO, JERRY," I MUTTERED to myself, "What are you hiding?"

The access times for the news drops were almost exactly a week old. Figuring a twenty-four hour news cycle for anything hot, and looking at the publications he'd dropped to, I figured that the story he was seeding had to have run on Monday, and been something locally based, and been pretty damn explosive to boot. Something with national impact. Something to do with corruption or civil liberties or foreign policy or something like that.

I searched the headlines in *The Mercury News*, and then searched those against *The Intercept* and *The Washington Post*.

I got my first hit in *The Intercept*:

San Jose Police Commissioner Implicated in Cover-Up

The copy read:

Deputy Commissioner Cyril Pullman declined to answer questions this morning about a series of photographs leaked to The Intercept that seem to place him at the scene of four recent police shootings, before the appearance of investigative staff.

In the opinion of this reporter, these photographs raise troubling questions about the already inexcusable trend of escalating police violence around the Bay in an era when violent crime, and indeed property crime, is at an all time low.

Further revelations are promised in the coming days...

And so on.

Further revelations. Had these leaks come from Jerry? What was his source? Was he at the scene of these shootings? Did he have recordings or video? Or had he broken into the SJPD system and looted confidential information?

Or all of the above?

Well, it gave me something to search for. A date range, if nothing else. I took the date of the most recent shooting—only a month ago—and searched for new documents, archives, photos, and videos since that date.

I struck gold.

The completely unsexy thing about this line of work is that, while you might get out into the open air to burn down forests and kill the occasional mercenary, most of it is just like any other job. You're stuck behind a computer or looking at papers, and trying to reconcile column A with column B.

But when column A contains the name of one of the most powerful people around the bay, and column B contains a dash-cam video of him participating in the cover-up of a shooting that was patently a murder...

Well, now I knew. Cyrill Pullman was enabling wanton slaughter, for reasons I couldn't even begin to fathom. And there had to be other people involved to, to afford the kinds of mercenaries I'd dealt with yesterday and this morning. Stillwater's one of the world's biggest private militaries, and their services don't come cheap.

They're also not supposed to be able to operate within the U.S.

This was Cal's case. When the gunmen were searching Francine, they were looking for the file he sent me to deliver—they expected the civvies to have it, or I was on their hit list, too.

And they knew where my house was.

"Nya! Get dressed! Grab Klepto."

"What's up?"

"We're not safe here. Get in the car. Drive to Reno. Take the prepaid debit cards. Hold up in a hotel room at the Peppermill until I call you for the all clear."

She popped her head in from the other room while I was closing everything up and stowing it away. "We have clients. I can't leave them in the..."

"Take anything you need. We should be safe in a

couple days. But don't take your phone. Take a prepaid. And don't use your cards, at all." Bad enough that she has to use her own car... "Actually, take the rental, too. No records, no trail. Disappear. I'll find you there in a couple days."

"What did he tell you last night?"

"Stillwater, the mercenary company. I've just found out what they're after, and none of us are safe until I blow it up."

"Blow it up?"

"You know what people will go through to cover up a crime."

"Ah, yeah, I have an idea."

"This is a doozy."

"So you have to release it to the public?"

Sometimes, I wonder why I bother to get out of bed in the morning. If Rachael ever comes back, she and Nya could run the agency without me and nobody would ever notice. "Not what I had in mind, but that'd do it."

"So why go to Reno? Why not go to Mount Hamilton?"

"Nya..." I raised an eyebrow at her, "I think I ought to give you a raise."

She didn't care like Rachael would have, but she smiled anyway.

Small victories, right?

MOUNT HAMILTON, ONE OF THE Bay Area's three major volcanoes, and the only one that still has active vents. Mount Diablo and its predecessor up in Tilden park had both packed it in a few eons ago and settled into their rocking chairs for a good solid retirement.

Mount Hamilton is all park and ranch land, except for an observatory, a translator station, and a discreet little palace that makes Hearst Castle look modest.

Earl Whitaker made his first fortune inventing the universal remote control. He made his second one in the crypto wars. He's never told me where he made his third, but with the hints he's dropped, I figure he must've gotten some good dirt on a few politicians along the way. His compound is what happens when Liberace gets hired to direct the marriage of CIA headquarters and Skullcrusher Mountain. It would take a SEAL team to breach in, and it would take ground-penetrating radar to find out where he went to hide while the groundpounders were breaking in through all the defenses. If those Stillwater fucks went after Nya and Klepto up here, they'd be in for a series of very unpleasant surprises.

Hell, the only reason I ever got in there the first time is that I was delirious, framed for murder, and had nowhere else to turn—and Earl owed me a favor.

I ran into him a couple times as a cop, but I didn't really learn how good he was at what he did until I ran down the anonymous tip that helped me nail the Broadway Slasher—my last major collar before they kicked me off the force.

Turned out he'd given me the tip because he wanted to embarrass the FBI agent who was leading the case. It worked. That guy runs a gas station now.

That's how I found him. Or, at least, how he found me. Then he showed up at that New Years' Eve party a couple years back...well, that's a long story. But it ended with him owing me, bigtime. So, even though we're technically even, I can get away with leaning on him a little.

Now that he's got more money than most deities, he hangs out behind the walls of his fortress and does what he wants. In Earl's case, that means cute college boys, secret collecting, and data mining.

To be honest, I suspect he'd do the data mining for free. Yeah, his prices do fall somewhere in the expanse between "arm," "leg," and "spleen," but he doesn't need the money—what he does need is a way to keep the riff-raff away.

Well, this morning, he wasn't getting off that easy.

I took my time collecting some presents for him from Stanford-UCSF, then took them down the Peninsula, across Sunnyvale, and up the mountain with Nya riding shotgun and Klepto in the back seat. There isn't anyone else I'd trust them with for the duration.

Did some sweet-talking at the gate. Spotted a couple illegal sentry robots with live guns in the lee of the guardhouse when we drove in. New upgrades. There are some transvestites you don't fuck with or they'll put you in stitches—Earl's up there on the list just above Eddie Izzard. One of these days, I expect the two of them will co-fund a bakery chain called "Cake or Death," with Izzard supplying the cake recipes.

"Clarkie, sweetie," he says when he opens the door, "What kinda gerbil fuckery is this?" Don't let him calling me 'sweetie' fool you. Or the fact that he was wearing pink high heels, a leather micro-mini, a rhinestone-studded dog collar, and a horse-tail. Despite the festive getup and the friendly language, he was not happy to see me. Last time I came by I was being framed for murder and had a machine-gun-toting mercenary on my tail. In his book, I'm the bringer of bad news and bad people. Not the kind of guy you want to bring around for tea.

"Don't worry," I said, "You're gonna love this."

"The hell, you say." He looked skeptically at Jerry, Lynn, and Palmer huddling in Palmer's Escort, parked next to Nya's MINI. Then he squinted at Nya and Klepto still sitting in the car, waiting for the all-clear. "Looks like you brought a fucking church social."

"Trust me, you're gonna love this." I pushed past him, waved the civvies in after me. "Got any coffee?"

WITH NYA AND KLEPTO OUTSIDE enjoying the midwinter sunset, I spent the next hour making introductions and convincing the Personae crowd to take Earl seriously, despite his affinity for crotchless leather underthings and the fact that he sits like a dude even when he's in drag.

Then, when they settled down enough to be willing to talk turkey, I brought up the hit team in the room—metaphorically speaking—and laid out what I'd found on Jerry's machine.

Lynn, predictably, went ape-shit, along the lines of "You swore you'd lay off the activism while we were doing business you stupid selfish short-sighted son of a bitch!" Than came round with another salvo when she realized that they'd been targeted as a pair because someone had traced the leaks back to an IP address at the company offices in Richmond.

I let it play itself out. Once all parties had exhausted their outrage, and Earl was giving me the kind of eye that said I'd better have something good up my sleeve or he was never putting up with my sorry ass again, I laid out my cunning plan.

"...Earl invests in your company for a controlling interest, and you do what he says to make this a viable business." I explained how he'd already generated billions and how he'd already done a lot of work in the open source space, "and in return for him doing you this favor, you're going to give him all the footage of the police cover ups you've got. You're going to give him your sources. All the info. Everything. And he's going to release them in a media blitz that can't be traced back to him or you, and that'll take the monkey off your back. Once everyone knows the secret, nobody has any reason to try to kill you."

"Hmph," Jerry snorted. "What about r...r...re...venge?"

"That's not how this kind of thing works. If they kill you before you release, they've covered their ass. Killing you afterwards just exposes them more. No, trust me, I've seen a lot of screwy shit around here. There's a logic to how it works. Anyone who comes after you for payback will wait a while, till they're clear themselves. By that time, you should all be rich enough to disappear anywhere you want to, if you decide you need to. Right, Earl?"

Earl just smiled that Cheshire-cat smile.

"So, if this is an agreeable setup to everyone, I'll leave you to work out the details."

ONE LOOK AT JERRY'S STASH of incriminating documents and Earl started getting all kinds of perverse ideas about how to rake the SJPD across the coals. It didn't take much more convincing.

I moved to get out of their way, so Earl walked me to the door. Once we were out of earshot he made it pretty clear that he wanted to have my babies. A nice change of pace—normally I want to have his, and it costs me a lot. This time, it turns out, I might even get a finder's fee.

He also wanted to make sure we were all safe. Something about the look on my face didn't make him all that happy. So I gave him a quick low-down on what had been going on and what I had planned next.

"I've only got one stipulation, Earl." I said, bringing it back around to business. "I want this on every news channel by midnight tonight. I want there to be no more reason for my clients to be a target."

"Oh, my sweet boy," Earl said, "it's a lovely theory, and you sold it like the Big Bad Wolf himself. But you forget the petty dictator's taste for vengeance. Why, there was this one woman at my first company..."

"I'm betting if we get this out in the open, and fast, they'll be too busy doing damage control, and they'll need every spare dollar for their lawyers."

"Ah, such childish optimism. Tell me, what did Calico say?"

"He said they weren't going to make it past the first round. Not the right people, not the right kind of experience. Interesting tech, but they were going about it all wrong. Why?"

"Don't you get your testicles in a knot over that, just get down the mountain and do what you gotta do."

"Them?" I nodded past him at the Personae folks who were on the couch.

"I'll leave 'em wet and happy and begging for more, promise. You keep your head down, cutie pie. Don't want it shot off when you're not looking. Here," he pushed something into my hand, then waved over my shoulder to Nya, who was playing fetch with Klepto in the front garden, "Get this activated on your main line and leave the Neanderthal with me. Call me when you've got the all clear, I'll come over for dinner."

I looked at my hand. He'd given me a phone. A kind

of phone you couldn't get anymore, because anytime a batch of them came out, the government bought them all up for their intelligence agents.

A Blackphone. The kind of phone that not even the NSA can snoop on, if you're using it right.

I stopped at a handy dandy cell phone outlet store to get it activated after I got down the mountain.

By the time I filled Nya in, said goodbye to Klepto, and got back in the car, the first bits of news were already coming in on the radio. I called Earl.

"You work fast."

"Well, what can I say? My favorite gumshoe always lightens my loafers."

"Earl, if your loafers get any lighter, you'll turn into a pineapple."

"Keep it up and I'm gonna invite you to my Halloween party."

I never know how to take Earl except when he's being very serious. I think he likes it that way. I do my best to make sure he doesn't know how to take me either.

A good man to have in your back pocket, though, so long as you don't mind being in his.

Now that I didn't have to worry about Nya, and my clients were as safe as I could make them, I could turn my attention to thornier business.

Like breaking into Cal Oldman's house.

5:40 PM, FRIDAY

THE OLDMANS LIVED IN A generous old-style carriage house in southeastern San Jose, not far from the Los Gatos border. Probably cost a hundred thousand dollars when they moved in—easily worth north of a million now. Gotta love Bay Area real estate.

Rachael's mother wouldn't be home until six thirty, at least if I remembered her schedule right. Cal, on the other hand, was due home any minute. I called him to ask, said I needed to talk to him later on this evening and wanted to figure out whether it was worth braving traffic in order to get down here at a civilized hour.

I slipped in the sliding glass door around the back. I had just enough time to find his office and paw through his desk, but he was too smart to keep any paper records where I could find them, at least not on this kind of truncated timetable, so it was going to have to be the direct approach.

My ass planted itself in the dining room table with a clear view of the front door, took out my .45, and waited in the gloom.

The light flicked on. Cal's weapon was out of his

holster before I even brought mine up from the table. I'd have to work on that.

"Hello, Cal."

"Lantham," he let his breath out and re-sheathed the weapon. "What the fuck?"

"I need to know what's in the envelope."

"This is a home invasion. Armed incursion into the home of a sworn officer of the law. You understand what that means."

"It means that I must want answers pretty bad, doesn't it?" I peaked an eyebrow at him.

"Sparks always said you had a thing for theatrics." Sparks is his pet name for Rachael—his daughter and my AWOL partner.

"Well, she doesn't tend to lie a lot."

Cal Oldman covered the distance between us in about a step or two more than I could have. Not his fault that I got lucky in the legs department, just a good thing to know. If you're going to hang out with a cop, you want to know if you might be able to outrun him in a pinch.

I kicked a tumbler across the table to him. "Single malt?"

He inclined his head. I poured a couple fingers each. Macallan Special Reserve. Good stuff. I figured the lubricant would loosen his tongue.

"What was in the envelope, Cal?"

"You don't want to know."

"Oh, I think we know better than that. I didn't get into a line of work where I get paid for being a nosy bastard for my health."

"Hmph. Quite the opposite, from what I hear."

"Yeah, I've heard that too. My doctor won't shut up about it. She stays up long nights worrying that my insurance will cancel my ass." I took a sip. Good scotch. Smoother on the tongue than any woman I've ever known, and that's saying something. "So make with the info. What's in the envelope? And what does it have to do with all these odds and ends you've had me running around for?"

"What does Revell Fender mean to you?"

"Not a thing."

"It should."

"Why?"

"Silicon Valley is the center of the world right now. You might have heard."

"I think I caught it on a TED talk."

"Yeah, well," he took a slug of the scotch. "It's not going to last, and everyone knows it. Unless."

"Unless what?"

"Unless some things change."

"And you're aiming to change them."

"Me? I'm just a civil servant who bought a house back when that was something you could do around here."

"Stop dancing, Cal."

"Sorry, Lantham," he dug down deep into his pocket, pulled out his phone, "But it's an internal matter. I'm just helping San Jose bust a few dirty cops, cause their IA people don't have any funding, so they can't even investigate cops that shoot civilians for the fun of it anymore..." He cradled his phone in his open palm, like it was a palmed playing card. He twitched it back and forth like he was waving it at me, then he set it down on the table, flat. "It's the kind of thing I thought you could get behind, but it *is* confidential."

I picked up what he was putting down. "I understand. Guess I oughta get going. I parked around back, do you mind...?"

"No, not at all."

I stood up, took my phone out, opened it up and pulled the battery. Then, just for good measure, I set it down on the table next to his. Cal expected that people were listening. He was right—every commercial phone but one—the one I'd just activated on the way here, thanks to Earl—is a listening device, and anyone with the right hacking chops can turn on the mic and listen remotely, anytime.

You can't do that with a Blackphone, but I didn't know if he'd recognize it, and this wasn't the time.

Then we took a walk. With the scotch. The early night air cooled enough that I was actually glad I brought my jacket. San Jose has two seasons: summer, and oven. Summer runs from October through May. Oven gets the rest of the year. Sometimes, even in the summer, you actually want sleeves.

Rather than wait for him to start talking, I opened with something that had been niggling at me all day. "Does the name Boswell ring any bells?"

"Bos...not sure. It might. I can to get back to you on that. Why?"

"Heard it a couple times up on that mountain today, in

connection with the hit."

"Interesting."

"Stop playing cagey, buddy, and spill. We're out here where no one can eavesdrop on us. You said something about change."

"Yeah. So, I think someone wants to change things...A few someones. And they've got fingers in a lot of pies around here."

"So what?" Changing things is kind of the local religion.

"'So what' is that things don't work this way anymore."

Cryptic much? "Cal, I swear to god..."

"How well do you keep up?"

"With what, tech?"

"Yeah."

"Well enough. If I don't, I'm out of a job."

"What's the one thing—the only thing—that matters in tech?"

"Moore's law."

"And in the four-step disruption curve, what's the last consequence of Moore's law?"

"Democretization. Access becomes ubiquitous. Money, power, special leverage, it all collapses. Why the pop quiz?"

"Who do you think might want to change that?"

Something shivery ran up the inside of my esophagus. "I can think of a zillion, but it's not like they can do anything about it. That ship sailed."

"It's not just Intel or Apple and Google, Lantham. Or the Cloud, or the biotech. It's FarSight, Palantir, Systems

Analysis Foundry, Project Trojan..."

"Wait, wait, what are you telling me?"

"When you went after Martin Galloway's killer, you stepped right next to a landmine we've been sitting on for a while."

"What's that?"

"I mentioned Revell Fender."

"Never heard of him."

"Wish I hadn't. Last year you helped the FBI recover a Chinese state treasure..."

"Yeah, stolen from the Cal Academy..."

"You had some business six months before involving the murder of some girls in Danville, and a Doctor Richard Sternwood..."

"Yeah, that's how I got Nya."

"And six months ago you investigated the suicide of venture capitalist Martin Galloway."

"What of it?"

"Revell Fender was an investor in Systems Analysis Foundry that supplied the augmented reality technology that got used in the Academy heist. He did a lot of business with Martin Galloway and is one of the big wigs who's suing to break the trust and seize control of Project Trojan. And he was the man behind the Oxford Group."

"The Oxford Group?"

"The ones that Charles Sternwood hooked up with at Harvard. The ones that tried to kill Nya Thales."

I kept my face straight and calm. Because if this Fender guy had that kind of reach... "What's his game?"

"That's what we need to find out. For the last two

years, we've been working on the same case from opposite ends. When Rachael told me some of what you were into, I knew we'd eventually have to talk."

"What's your interest?"

"Besides the whole cop thing?"

"Besides that, yeah."

"Fender is connected to old institutions that are used to the old-world way of doing things. The kind that start wars and kill people to protect industries, because it's in the public interest. If the old world goes away like it's already started to..."

"Then the people who built it might do anything to bring it back."

"These are people that build nuclear weapons, Clarke. They're the people who weaponized smallpox and VX. These aren't the kind of people you want trying to prove they're needed. And they've been putting a lot of pieces into play around the Valley, and in my department. And I think they're going to make a big move, sometime soon."

"Unless we can get ahead of them."

We'd made it most of the way around the block. Cal stopped, looked me up and down. "You've got eight years on your service record."

"Yeah?"

"Another two an you get your lifetime federal weapons permit."

"So?"

"So how would you like a job? Long term. Working for me. Officially. Independent IA auditor, full Deputy status."

"I still keep the agency?"

"You'd be useless to me if you didn't."

"Let me think about it."

11:00 PM, SUNDAY

I THOUGHT ABOUT IT. For a long time. It's not the kind of job you just blunder into, even when you've got my sense of style and make a career of blundering into things.

Didn't help that it was the kind of thing I felt like I'd been building to my whole life. I grew up in the mountains above Santa Cruz, where the world-saving gene runs high in every single nut and flake in the whole place. It's the kind of sexy that you can't buy. The kind that powers all the craziness that powers this whole crazy area.

So I took walks at night when everyone else was asleep. Because the one thing I really wanted to do, the one thing that really would have made a difference, I couldn't.

When you're making a decision that could put everyone you love in danger, you're supposed to talk to them. That's the deal. That's what you do, if you've got an ounce of decency in your soul.

If you've even got a soul.

But I couldn't. Rachael was gone. Nya...I didn't even

know how to begin to bring it up with Nya.

Erica came back on Saturday morning, couldn't tell me where she'd been. I couldn't talk to her either, couldn't tell her what was up. How could I? If Cal was right, and I joined his little revolution, I could well find myself going up against elements inside the FBI.

The term "conflict of interest" might have been hanging in my mind if I'd been thinking more clearly.

But I wasn't. I wasn't thinking much at all, except on those late night walks. I was stupidly happy to be alive after a week like this, and to have made it clear of the whole ugly business with Jerry and Lynn and Palmer and the mercenaries without losing a client or a Klepto or a kindred spirit. I just wanted to settle down and enjoy a quiet life. You know the kind of thing? A little barbecue here, a little sex with my girlfriend there, some wrestling games with the mutt, some misty-eyed wistful musings on how great this house would feel with a few kids in it...

It was enough to make me want to pass over Cal's proposal as a bad idea.

Because it was, you know. A bad idea.

A really bad idea.

The kind of idea that can turn your world upside down and shake until everyone falls out who can't hang on for dear life.

The kind of idea you don't let fester in your head if you want to live a long and healthy life.

By Sunday evening, I'd gotten over the sex appeal of joining a rebellion against the system. I had plenty of other sexy things to distract me. Erica was *very* happy to see me, and the feeling was mutual. We'd fallen behind on our mutual reading project in the three weeks she'd been off on assignment, and since she still wasn't allowed to tell me anything about what had been going on, we built a fire in the fire pit out back, pulled up a couple hammocks, and read passages of our book to each other by the firelight...well, after we got tired of naked oil wrestling. That was fun too.

We even managed to roast a few sausages that Klepto didn't get his choppers on before we ate them.

And let me tell you something, as nice as reunions are, as gorgeous as that evening was, as wonderful as Erica smelled, as comfortable as it felt to touch her again, none of it held a candle to how fine it was to hear her reading Jules Verne, out loud, in a very convincing French accent.

"You know," I said, leaning from my hammock toward her. "I don't think there's anyone I'd rather be stranded at the center of the Earth with."

"Not even Klepto?"

"Oh, we'd have to take Klepto along. He'd hold off the dinosaurs." I kissed her. "I'm gonna go get an IPA, want one?"

"More in a Lambic mood."

"Think I've got some of that, too. Be right back." I jogged inside, decided to hit the bathroom before I got the drinks. While I was in there, my phone buzzed. I'd left it in the kitchen.

I flushed and crossed the floor from the little bathroom at the top of the stairs. The caller ID gave me a number I'd never heard of from somewhere up in Shasta County, but I was already in here and my gun-toting redhead was out by the fire with a dangerous animal, so I answered it anyway. You never know when it might be a client.

"Clarke Lantham Investigations. This is Lantham, what problem can I solve?"

"Lantham?"

My heart jumped straight up and started throbbing at the back of my throat. I thought I was going to choke. My eyes got misty and I blinked 'em away as fast as I could. I didn't say anything for a full minute.

She just breathed on the other end of the line.

I opened the TV room window, which overlooks the patio, and waved to Erica, mouthing "Client" in big unsubtle motions. She nodded.

Me? I fled out the front door and headed out to the street. I figured, this time of night, I wasn't likely to get picked up for walking around in shorts and a t-shirt, even if they technically were god-awful *Monty Python* boxer shorts which claimed my butt crack was just a flesh wound.

"Lantham? Are you there?" Her voice was quiet, almost like she didn't want anyone to find out she was calling.

My stomach felt like someone had kicked it in. I didn't know whether to apologize or start yelling again.

"Rachael?" I walked fast as I could, hooked a right at Lorena and then slowed to a stroll in front of the duplex on the corner. Off the main drag it was quieter, and I wouldn't have to shout in case of traffic. "What the hell..."

"I'm sorry. This was a bad idea."

"I'm sorry too. For the other day."

"I deserved it. Shit. Fuck. I should just go, I didn't mean to interrupt. I just...you know."

"Not really."

"Forget it then. I...just...Mom said you were asking about me."

"Where are you?"

"Doesn't matter. I'll be gone before you get here. I'm...I'm okay, is all. Okay? Don't come looking for me."

She sounded like she was trying to keep her voice under control. She was doing a damn good job, but I've been in enough tight scrapes with her to know what she sounds like when she's three inches away from losing her shit.

"Why would I do that? You bailed."

"This...this was a bad idea."

"This is the second time this week, Rache. What's up?"

"I'm...I'm sorry. I'll...just, whatever you do, don't come looking for me, okay?"

And the phone went dead. Something inside me went dead too. Couldn't figure out what it was.

It was warm out there. The street was quiet. It was the kind of place that felt like home anytime you relaxed and just let it. Last time I'd been on this street with Rachael, taking a stroll for a bit of a management consult, she'd been antsy. She wouldn't tell me why. Then, a few days later she'd up and disappeared, right after risking her life to save mine.

Now I was out there alone. And it didn't seem like it really mattered that Erica was back home by that fire waiting for me to finish reading with her, to take her to bed, to start talking about maybe planning a wedding. Everything that made sense five minutes ago made less than no sense now.

Lantham, what the hell are you doing with your life?

Out there, with nobody else in any direction, I felt like the last man on earth, and I didn't like it.

I fucking hated it.

Because I wasn't sure I knew who that schmuck was, that was standing out there on that street in the *Monty Python* boxer shorts. Looking at all those windows, still lit up with people inside, sharing movies and games, evenings and family time.

The kinds of things that I'd finally let myself start wanting. The kinds of things that, as long as there was an Oldman in my life, I'd never really get.

I used to like being alone—time was, I'd have done just about anything to get rid of Rachael, and Nya, and the whole ridiculous business. I liked being alone because I didn't have to deal with any bullshit.

But life didn't work that way anymore. Something about them, and Erica, and Klepto, had changed something about me. And I didn't know how life made any sense without them.

One thing's for sure, Lantham, I said to myself, *as long as Cal's mixed up in this crazy scheme, Rachael's going to be in the line of fire. And if she gets hurt, and you didn't do anything to stop it, you're going to lose everything.*

It would break Nya's heart. And mine.

People don't stop being family just because they run away. I might want to kill her, but that didn't mean I wanted to see her dead.

So I brought up the text window, punched in Cal Oldman's number.

Cal, remember that movie you were telling me about? I think I'd like to go see it.

And I hit "Send."

I was in. For keeps. Whatever it wound up costing.

The fire was still warm when I got back. Erica was snoozing in her hammock. I took the book from her and picked up reading. She stirred, and smiled, and I held her hand while Klepto curled up next to me in my hammock. I did my best southern accent, and it made her laugh.

But somehow, it wasn't the same.

The End
Clarke Lantham will return in
Blood and Weeds

EXTRAS

Author's Note

Once Clarke Lantham got involved with the police again, when Rachael got Cal Oldman to stick his neck out in *He Ain't Heavy*, it was only a matter of time before he got stuck in a sticky situation—and, being Lantham, it seemed only appropriate that that sticky situation involved him getting run off the road by an out-of-control truck. I've been on the bad end of that physics equation before, and in my case it ended well—a friendly passer-by pulled me out of the ditch, and I went on my way, none the worse for wear.

But if the accident had happened just ten yards further up the road (where there was a two-hundred-foot drop-off), or if the passer-by had been a touch less friendly, or if the guy who ran me off the road had run off the road right after me, it would have been a very different story.

It's a hell of a feeling being naked and alone (figuratively speaking), shorn of technology and oppressed by weather, out in the middle of the country. For a city boy, the first time it happens, it's downright terrifying. All I could think of for the twenty minutes that I stood in that deep ditch by the side of the road was "What if the wrong person stops to help? What if they killed me and took my ID and my car? Would anyone ever even know who I was?" At that point in my life, I'd never had any dental work done, and I didn't think they'd be able to identify me no matter how hard they tried.

Thankfully, the kindness of strangers proved my paranoid teenage brain was just racing ahead of itself, much like it always had. But that singular feeling of being stuck in the dark, alone, and utterly at the mercy of everything and everybody stuck with me.

And, eventually, it turned into the twisted love story that is *In The Cloud*.

Although they may not look like it on the surface, Clarke Lantham's adventures are love stories. Not, perhaps, for the characters, but for the author. Lantham's world is filled with things I have been in love with since before I can remember. Each view, each puzzle, most of the minor characters and villains, all of the cars, most of his hobbies, and a good number of the ideas for his cases all arise out of various insane passions I have rattling around in my brain.

Most of the time, when Lantham goes to a house, or looks at a view, or eats at a restaurant, you're seeing the real sights and sounds and smells of the Bay Area. The traffic patterns are real, the roads and geography, the politics and culture—it's all part of what makes that insane part of the world so ineffably captivating.

And, when I started the series, it was easy. If I got stuck on a point and needed to double-check a description, I could walk out my front door, hop into my convertible, and take the most interesting road I could lay tires on to go look at it.

This book is a little different. This is the first Lantham book that depends upon geography that does not technically exist. While the road, and the corner, that

Lantham got wrecked on are there for anyone to see, the features of the land around it are actually a composite of a couple river valleys in Watsonville and Marin County, while the mountain retreat and stable are based upon an estate in Boulder Creek that I once spent a week at.

But I trust you'll forgive me a little geographic license. It is, after all, only a novel—and, this time, for the first time, I'm writing without ready physical access to the geography. My retreat from that marvelous locale that gave shape to so many decades of life coincides with some other interesting shifts in the series, long-planned for.

This volume marks a major turning point in the Lantham series, one that's always been in the cards since I wrote the final scene in the first book—the title and the final line of which are both *And Then She Was Gone*. If you'll remember, during that book Lantham was being shadowed by a woman with a large gun and an indeterminate agenda, who ensured that, when the case was all wrapped up, there were no witnesses to corroborate Lantham's story about why anyone might want to murder Nya—and then someone working with her warned Lantham to stay away from the case, or else.

Lantham's reticence is the price he's had to pay for Nya's safety, all this time. But this is Lantham, and he's not going to be able to leave it alone forever. Especially not now that this group has a name, and is showing up connected to his other cases. As he uncovers more connections between his life and The Oxford Group...well, let's just say that I'm really excited to see how it all unfolds. The one thing I, as the author, am sure about is that somewhere along the line, one or more of these characters is going to screw up my master plan, and leave me scrambling to find out what happens next.

But that's okay. The times that try Lantham's soul are always good for mine. The guy is just so damn much fun to torture I can't help myself.

I hope you enjoyed yourself, and that you'll join me next time as Lantham takes a job from his ten-year-old neighbor and winds up in the midst of a predicament more twisted than anything he's seen so far—with implications reaching far beyond the fate of the boy, his father, and the university he works for.

Keep your eyes peeled. It's a weird world out there.

-J. Daniel Sawyer
Lincoln City, Oregon
July 8, 2015

Blood and Weeds
A Clarke Lantham Mystery
Sneak Preview

1:00 AM, FRIDAY

"CLARKE, JESUS, YOU'LL WAKE up everyone." Erica barely said it without laughing herself. She had to bite her knuckles to do so, one of the little things she does that breaks that cool-as-steel FBI facade they trained into her at Quantico. Kinda like watching a tiger get all cuddly when you give it a beach ball. And she wonders why I put up with her work schedule.

Silly tiger.

"Serve you right, to get hauled in for disturbing the piece." I kept my voice low so it didn't, in fact, wake up everyone in the houses we were walking past. "You think Nya could bail us out? Or would we have to call Rivers?" That would be Special Agent-in-Charge Ronald Rivers, for those of you joining this torrid tale in progress. Her boss, and apparently born with an abnormal affection for alliteration. After his parents saddled him with initials that make him feel at home at every railroad crossing in America, he went and hired Erica Ellis as his chief advancement agent on special assignments, and one time when I got her drunk enough she let slip that there was a Leslie Lawrence and a Daniel Dartmouth on the team too.

She flared her eyebrows at me. "If you ever so much as..."

"Cross my heart, hope to die, stick a thousand needles in my eye," I tried to hold up my right hand, but Klepto was pulling, so I had to switch his leash before making with the solemnity. "I wouldn't dream of it."

"Be careful when you say that. You talk in your sleep."

Well, she's right, I do. I've recorded it. I sound like an aphasic who's been filled with the Holy Spirit. Probably a good thing. My dreams aren't something I'd willingly inflict on an enemy, much less a bed mate.

"You didn't read the part of the license agreement where it says 'listen at your own risk.'" I smiled at her. She smiled at me. Sometimes, that's all it takes to make a too-warm summer night into something special.

Or, at least, I thought so. Sir Klepto the Maniac, my teenaged pit bull-mastiff cross, had other ideas. For him, it takes a really interesting tree, or fire hydrant, or—in this case—juniper bush, overgrown with African daisies and filled with interesting urine deposits and little creatures he can chase. When he was a puppy, not that long ago, all it took to make him ignore the canine community bulletin board and come to heel was an encouraging noise. Now, it took a stout leash and a goodly amount of patience. Another year or so, and he'd be all grown up, and subduing bad guys by drowning them with kisses.

I clicked my cheek and jiggled the leash. "Klepto, come on. Leave the daisies alone. That's not your flower bed."

He looked back and whined at me. I cocked my

eyebrow, which he took as some kind of permission, and dove back into the bush.

"Aieee!" The bush seemed to have an opinion about this.

"Um..." That's me being intelligent at one in the morning. Impressive, eh?

"Who's there?" Erica was all business. Reached for her gun, which she wasn't wearing, then rolled her eyes at herself.

A shame. There ain't a lot sexier in the world than a redhead with a gun.

"Just me. It's just me." A hand poked out of the bush, a little hand. Not easy to see whose hand it was in the as-dark-as-it-gets-in-the-suburbs.

And I knew the voice. "Teddy? That you?"

"Yeah. Yeah, Mister Lantham, it's me. Ow!"

"Who? Wait..." Erica said, "Is this the kid from..."

"Yeah." Neighbor kid from three houses down. We met when I asked him to stop doing rail slides on the retaining wall at the front of my yard, on the grounds that I had a migraine and didn't want to get arrested for shooting a child in the head. After that, he started shadowing me. Evidently, when you're ten, having a private detective in the neighborhood is the next best thing to living next to a spy or a Nazi war criminal. I gave up and decided to like him when he opened up his own detective agency catering to the other kids in the neighborhood, and started coming by for consults on Saturday afternoons. "Teddy, what are you doing out at this hour?"

"I snuck out." He climbed out between the branches, came out covered in crumbs and prickles from the juniper bark. He wasn't more than ten, I'd didn't know for sure cause I'd never actually asked him his age, and he never volunteered it. He seemed to think that if he didn't mention that he was less than twenty-five, I wouldn't notice.

"Won't you get in trouble?"

"Not if you don't turn me into the Gestapo."

"Hell of a thing to call your mother. Teddy Stride, this is Erica Ellis, Special Agent with the FBI."

His eyes went big as saucers. "FBI? Really?"

She nodded. "Really."

"Are you Mister Lantham's big squeeze?"

She chuckled. "Big squeeze?"

"Well, that's what Nya calls you."

"You know Nya too? That can't be safe..." She gave me the kind of look that said *You've explained to her about the age of consent, I assume.* Erica has some pretty traditional ideas about relationships, and she thinks anyone that has Nya's ideas about them must be a barely-contained sexual danger to self and others.

Which goes to show you that even really fabulous people can be a bit dippy around the edges.

"It's *fine.*" It was my turn to roll my eyes, and not really care is she saw. She wasn't going to pick a fight about it in front of the kid, and it was now officially on my list of things to talk over with her at length and over bourbon.

"Yeah, she's great. Why?"

"Forget it, Ted. It's a thing."

"You say that a lot..."

"Hmph." Erica was still smiling through the harrumph, which I took to be a good sign. "You've got no idea."

"Ted, dude, why are you out?"

"Oh! Well...um..." It's never a good sign when a kid like this goes sheepish.

"You're screwing up my date. If I don't get laid tonight it's your fault..."

"Clarke..." Note to self: Don't mention sex in front of the girlfriend and the prepubescent at the same time. She has a thing about that, something she calls 'propriety.' My mother used to use that word sometimes, and I still don't think she knew what it meant. Erica doesn't either.

"...so make with the syllables, or I will call the Gestapo."

"Okay, okay, just...look, can we talk in your office?" He was looking around like he was afraid the fence might overhear him.

"Why?"

"Well...I kinda need to hire you."

I sighed. "Look, Teddy, really, just come by this Saturday and I'll consult like usual..."

"No, no, it's not that. It's..." He stopped talking, closed the distance between us, then stood on his toes and whispered in the general direction of my head, which was in orbit a few miles above his. "It's my Dad. Something's wrong with him."

"Like, medically?"

"No. Like, I think he saw something...awful."

"Like what?"

"Like somebody got beat up. Or killed maybe."

I blinked. Then I did it again just to make sure that my eyes were still there.

"Where?"

"At work."

"Teddy...he works at a college." He didn't just work at a college, he worked at Sanderson Bible College over in the City, which is only a little bit less uptight and freaked out than a traffic warden who's been strapped to the front of a stock car on free beer night. People that boring don't commit murder, except by euthanizing their congregations with deeply probing readings of bible verses like Deuteronomy 23:12.

Okay, so I spent a little time in Vacation Bible School when I was thirteen. In my defense, it was the only way for a good Catholic boy to have any chance at kissing the cute girls from the Baptist church across the road.

"I know. But there's things going on there. Big things, and I ain't supposed to tell anyone, but..." He looked at me with this kind of solemn panic, like he was willing me to believe, and willing me to believe I was the only hope.

"All right, kid, you got yourself a snoop. Do you mind if the Fed listens in? It's not technically in her jurisdiction, but she might have some tips."

Teddy squinted at her, like he was trying to get the size of her. "I guess so."

"Well, then, best way to stay ahead of spies is to keep walking. Come on." I coaxed Klepto back onto the sidewalk, and the four of us crowded the place up.

It's about half a mile around the block I live on. Klepto'd ferreted out our interloper about halfway down the first leg, so we had plenty of time to talk.

"It started last month. Dad stopped coming home until real late, after Mom was in bed. Didn't matter how late she stayed up, he just wouldn't come home. Like he was circling or something, waiting for her light to go out, you know? Well, they got in a fight, and I heard it cause I stayed up to find out what was going on. He was saying we had to move, cause the school's moving to Red Bluff. It's a lot cheaper up there, you know? We could buy a house and everything, maybe even have a horse!

"But Mom wasn't happy about it. Dad talked and talked, trying to convince her, but the more he talked the more it sounded like he was scared, not happy.

"Well, the next morning he was gone again, and wouldn't come back for anything. Even when I called. And he kept doing that. Just never coming home."

I didn't make the obvious observation, but I shared a look with Erica. She thought the same thing I did, but how do you tell a fifth grader from a conservative home that his father's cheating on his mother?

Instead, I said "How does that add up to him seeing someone get killed?"

"That wasn't how I found out. Duh."

"So how did you find out?"

"Well, it was last night. I got up to go to the bathroom, and, well, you know how our back bathroom has that window that looks out on the lawn, right?"

"Yeah." I'd never actually been to his house, but he'd

told me about how it was one of his favorite escape hatches before. His family's back yard stretches half the length of the block, so if he wants to get to anywhere in the neighborhood, all he has to do is get out to the back of the house, run out to the yard, and hop the fence into an apartment complex parking lot. Since his parents sleep at the front of the house, they never know he's gone on his secret missions. That setup's gonna serve him really well in a couple years when he finds out about girls and creative driving and all the other fun ways you can get in trouble when you're in high school.

"Well, I was looking out while I was taking a leak, and I see him out there in the back yard, just sitting on the tire swing. All bent over, you know? I mean, you know Dad, you know he never does that."

"Sure." Tom—his father—actually had a generally depressive air about him, but he was one of those stiff-upper-lip types who didn't want anyone to see anything but the smiling veneer.

"Well, I went out to see what was wrong. I took my phone, like you taught me. I recorded it. Glad I did too, cause wow..."

"Hey, wait a second," Erica said, "Did you ask him if you could record him?"

"No, of course not."

I could feel Erica's eyes drilling a disapproving hole in the side of my head. "You know it's a felony in California to record someone without their knowledge, right? It's called wiretapping, and they can send you to jail for it."

"But you do it all the time Mister..."

"That's because I'm an idiot." I risked a glance up to Erica. Yeah, I was in trouble. I decided to hold off on explaining how to decide which laws are flexible and how to avoid getting caught until we were safely away from Federal surveillance. "I'll explain later. You got the phone with you?"

"Sure."

"Mind if I borrow it? I'll give it back tomorrow."

"Okay..."

"Come over, say, four o'clock. After school..."

"It's summer vacation."

"Okay, so come over at two. I'll give you your phone back, we'll talk."

"I've only got twenty bucks."

"We'll figure something out."

"So you'll take the case?"

"If what's on that recording squares with what you're telling me, I'll think about it."

We shook on it. He slipped me his phone, then ran ahead to get back in bed before the Gestapo did a bed check. Before he was even around the next corner, Erica said:

"You shouldn't be toying with that boy that way, you know."

"Who's toying?"

"You can't possibly think he's serious."

"Sweetheart, he just gave me his phone." I held up the non-too-cheap HTC. "He's serious."

"There's a difference between serious and right. What are you gonna do when you catch his father schtupping the secretary?"

"I'll figure it out. Trust me."

I can't be sure, but I think someone once said that right before getting hit by a train.

This ends this sample of
Blood and Weeds
Look for the full novel in 2016 wherever ebooks and paperbacks are sold

Also by J. Daniel Sawyer

The Antithesis Progression
Predestination and Other Games of Chance
Free Will
Avarice (forthcoming)

The Clarke Lantham Mysteries
And Then She Was Gone
A Ghostly Christmas Present
Smoke Rings
Silent Victor
He Ain't Heavy
In The Cloud
Blood and Weeds
The Bodies In The Basement
The Sky Miners (forthcoming)

Suave Rob's Amazing Adventures
Suave Rob's Double-X Derring-Do
Suave Rob's Rough-and-Ready Rugrat Rapture
Suave Rob's Amazing Ass-Saving Association

Standalone Works
Down From Ten
The Resurrection Junket
Ideas, Inc.
The Auto Motive (Forthcoming)

Collections
Sculpting God: Bedtime Stories for Adults
Frock Coat Dreams: Romances, Nightmares, and Fancies from
the Steampunk Fringe

Non-Fiction
The Every Day Novelist
Business 101
In Thirty Days (forthcoming)

Writer's Guides
Science Fiction Weaponry: A Guide for Writers (with Mary Mason)

Throwing Lead: A Writer's Guide to Firearms and the People Who Use Them (with Mary Mason)
Making Tracks: A Writer's Guide to Audiobooks and How to Produce Them

About the Author

With the advent of his hard-boiled Clarke Lantham Mysteries, J. Daniel Sawyer's abusive behavior toward the English language finally landed him in serious trouble, and he now spends his days and nights chained to a desk in a vain attempt to write his way out of the loony bin. Unfortunately, his attempts have yielded further entries in his sci-fi thriller series The Antithesis Progression, the cabin fever comedy Down From Ten, and significant alterations in his medication. On the rare occasion that he slips his bonds, he escapes to the wilds of the San Francisco back country where he devotes his energies to running afoul of local traffic ordinances in his never-ending pursuit of the ultimate driving road.

Should you be so inclined, you can communicate with this shady character, as well as find stories, podcasts, articles, and other literary abominations at http://www.jdsawyer.net

www.ingramcontent.com/pod-product-compliance
Lightning Source LLC
Chambersburg PA
CBHW021952170626
46808CB00001B/124